As Caroline got closer to her house, her heart leapt—Alex's car was parked out front! He was back early! She took the steps to the porch two at a time. When she got to the top, she saw that somebody was sitting on the floor of the porch—then she saw that it was *two* somebodies.

Alex was sitting on a beach blanket, next to Chrissy, who was wearing the tiniest bikini Caroline had ever seen. She couldn't see Alex's face but Chrissy's expression was impossible to miss—she was gazing at Alex in total adoration.

Caroline's heart hammered so loudly that she was sure both of them would hear it and turn around. But it was only too clear that they were oblivious to the world around them. Caroline watched as Alex patted Chrissy's hand and said, "So don't forget. It's a date, okay?"

"Okay," Chrissy began. Then she looked up and saw Caroline. Alex turned around and they both stared at her. Guilt was written all over their faces.

"Welcome home, Alex," Caroline said. "What a nice surprise."

Other series from Bantam Books for Young Readers
Ask your bookseller for the books you have missed

CAITLIN: THE LOVE TRILOGY created by
Francine Pascal
Loving
Love Lost
True Love

CAITLIN: THE PROMISE TRILOGY created by
Francine Pascal
Tender Promises
Promises Broken
A New Promise

CAITLIN: THE FOREVER TRILOGY created by
Francine Pascal
Dreams of forever
Forever and Always
Together Forever

ALL THAT GLITTERS by Kristi Andrews
1 *Magic Time*
2 *Take Two*
3 *Flashback*
4 *Love Lights*
5 *Typecast*

Two Girls, One Boy

BANTAM BOOKS
TORONTO • NEW YORK • LONDON • SYDNEY • AUCKLAND

For my mother and in memory of my father,
both of whom gave me a childhood
full of sugar and spice and all things nice.

TWO GIRLS, ONE BOY

A BANTAM BOOK 0 553 17565 3

First publication in Great Britain

PRINTING HISTORY
Bantam Books edition July 1988

Bantam Books are published by Transworld Publishers Ltd.,
61–63 Uxbridge Road, Ealing, London W5 5SA,
in Australia by Transworld Publishers (Aust.) Pty. Ltd.,
15–23 Helles Avenue, Moorebank, NSW 2170, and in New
Zealand by Transworld Publishers (N.Z.) Ltd., Cnr. Moselle
and Waipareira Avenues, Henderson, Auckland.

Printed and bound in Great Britain by
Hazell Watson & Viney Limited
Member of BPCC plc
Aylesbury Bucks

Prologue

Caroline

"So what's she like, my cousin Chrissy?" Caroline Kirby demanded. She was perched among the pillows on the high window seat in her parents' bedroom, and she gazed out at the pastel houses of the city and the San Francisco Bay while her mother unpacked suitcases.

Her mother looked up at her. She smiled. "Oh, a little like you, I think. Tall and slim like you are, although the way she eats, if it weren't for all the exercise she gets she'd be a blimp by now. Her hair's blond like yours—a bit lighter I think—and blue eyes. But she has freckles on her nose from being outside so much. Except for the freckles, you look very similar. In fact we came across some photos of my mother when she was young, and you both look a lot like her. . . ."

"So Grandma Hansen had blond hair, too?" Caroline asked.

Her mother smiled wistfully. "I remember how I always wished I had my mother's hair, because my father used to tell her it was spun gold. Spun gold on your head seemed like such a nice thing to have. And her hair was still almost the same color when she died. . . ." Caroline's mother's voice trailed off and she began to throw clothes into the hamper.

Caroline watched in silence for a while, afraid of saying the wrong thing. "Are you glad you went, Mom?" she asked at last.

Her mother gazed down at her hands for a long while without speaking.

"Yes, I am glad," she said at last. "It was painful for me to see my mother like that, but I'm glad we made our peace before she died."

"Going back must have been hard for you. After all those years cut off from your family."

Her mother sighed and pushed back her hair from her face. "For such a needless reason, too," she said. "They couldn't accept the man I wanted to marry, so they forced me to choose between my family and him."

Caroline looked up in amazement. Her mother had never spoken of the past so frankly before. All Caroline knew was that there had been a quarrel long before. She never imagined that the fight had been over her father.

"Is that Daddy we're talking about? They thought Daddy was unacceptable?" A picture of her quiet, scholarly father, shuffling around the house in slippers, his nose buried in a book, flashed through her mind.

She couldn't help a grin from twitching at the edges of her lips.

Her mother smiled, too. "He was a little different in those days," she said. "So was I. But I knew he was the right person for me. My mother was too narrow-minded to see that at the time and too stubborn to make the first move later. My sister Ingrid told me she talked about me a lot before she died. She said she wished things had been different."

"I wish they'd been different, too," Caroline said wistfully.

Caroline's mother nodded. "Of course you do," she said. "You've missed out on a lot having no close relatives around."

Caroline smiled. "I remember how jealous I was of Maria because she got the Girl Scout award for selling the most cookies. It wasn't even fair, because she sold them to all her uncles and aunts!"

Mrs. Kirby looked at her daughter with sympathy. "Maybe we can make up for that now," she said. "It was so good to see Ingrid and her family. I hadn't realized how much I missed my own sister all these years. To think that now she's married, with a family of her own. Little Ingrid, my kid sister, with four nearly grown children!"

"Including a cousin who's just the same age as me!" Caroline said. She slid from the window seat and danced across to her mother. "I can't wait to meet her. Can we take a trip out to Iowa sometime?"

"I don't think we'll need to do that," Caroline's mother said, smiling mysteriously. "If a little plan works out, you might see her very soon."

"A plan? What plan?" Caroline asked.

"My sister would like to send Chrissy to stay with us for the next school year," her mother said, putting her last pair of pantyhose into a drawer and shutting it firmly. "She's worried Chrissy is getting too serious about a boy at school, and she wants her to see what the rest of the world is like before she gets married and becomes a farmer's wife, too. So I suggested she spend a year with us."

Caroline stood like a statue, digesting this information. "A whole year?" she asked. "Where would she sleep?"

"She'd have to share your room," her mother said, hesitantly.

"Oh, come on, Mom," Caroline said, "I really don't think I want to share my room with a stranger for a year!"

"It will do you good," her mother said, smiling fondly. "You spend far too much time shut away in that room as it is. Besides, Chrissy's not a stranger. She's your cousin."

"But what if we don't like each other?" Caroline asked, her forehead creasing into a frown.

"You were just dancing around saying you were dying to meet her," her mother reminded her.

"I am dying to meet her," Caroline agreed. "I'd love to have her come and stay with us, but not for a whole year, Mother. Someone in my room for a year would drive me bananas!"

"I think you'll enjoy Chrissy," her mother said quietly. "She struck me as the sort of girl who's a lot of fun."

Caroline eyed her suspiciously. She stood there, playing with a white needlepoint pillow her mother had stitched. "But what about school?" she demanded. "Would she have to go to school with me?"

"Of course she would," her mother said. "That would be a major reason for her coming here. Chrissy is used to a small, rural high school where the selection of courses is poor. If she goes with you to Maxwell, she'll be exposed to lots of new ideas, and maybe she'll be more motivated to go to college."

Caroline moved away and knelt on the window seat again. A cable car was inching down the hill like a giant beetle, heading for Fisherman's Wharf. She could hear its bell clanging even through the closed window. She watched its progress while she tried to order her confused thoughts. A sequence of scenes ran through her brain—a strange girl taking up half the space in her room, walking with her to school, eating lunch with her friends.

When her mother had returned an hour earlier with news of a new cousin, Caroline had longed to meet her. She still wanted to meet her, but living with her for a whole school year was a very different matter. How would a farm girl from Iowa fit in to Caroline's life?

"I really don't think it would work, Mother," she said. "You know what Maxwell is like. It's a really tough college-prep school. We don't have any Mickey Mouse courses. And my friends—they're all pretty sophisticated. It would be embarrassing. They'd all be talking about the summer they spent in Europe, and Chrissy would be talking about her summer with the pigs."

"Don't be such a snob, Caroline," her mother said firmly. "Remember, I came from the very same farm town. Everybody in this world has something to learn from other people. From what I saw of Chrissy, she's a nice, bright girl and your friends will be happy to know her. I think you might have a lot to learn from her, too."

"Me?" Caroline squeaked, making an elaborate stage gesture toward herself with her hands. "What would I want to learn about farm life in Iowa? I really can't see any future for myself in slopping the hogs—whatever that means." She turned to her mother and grinned. Her mother smiled back.

"Why don't we have this conversation in a year's time," she said. "I think it might be very interesting to see exactly what you have learned from Chrissy."

"Does that mean she's definitely coming, whether I want her to or not?" Caroline asked.

"It certainly looks that way," her mother said. "They were going to talk it over today and call me tonight. All they have to do is to persuade Chrissy that coming here is a good idea—and what girl in her right mind would turn down a chance to come to California?"

Chrissy

"California?" Chrissy Madden shrieked. "You want me to go to California for a whole year?" She waved her arms in a gesture worthy of an opera singer about to plunge a dagger into her heart.

"But you just said you were dying to go to California." Her mother smiled. "You said you couldn't wait to meet your cousin Caroline and see a real ocean."

"But I meant go out for vacation," Chrissy said, climbing onto the arm of the well-worn, over-stuffed armchair where her mother was sitting. "I'd love to go out there for a vacation, but I wouldn't want to be away for a whole year. I'd never survive away from all of you and Ben."

"I know a year sounds like a long time, Honeybun," her mother said softly. "Believe me, when your Aunt Edith first suggested it, your dad and I didn't even take her seriously. I mean, a year is a long time to let your only little girl go off alone—especially to a big city like San Francisco. But as we talked about it, we came to realize what a wonderful chance it will be for you. We wouldn't want to deny you that chance." She turned to pat her daughter on the knee. "Think of it, Chrissy—you'll be able to go to a top high school, and you'll come back a sophisticated city girl just like your cousin Caroline."

Chrissy slid from the chair arm. "I don't want to come back a city girl," she said. "I want to be me, just the way I am now. My friends wouldn't know me. Ben wouldn't even like me anymore if I was a city girl."

"We just want you to realize that there is more to the world than Danbury, Iowa, so you can make the right decisions later," her father said calmly.

Chrissy did not miss the quick glance that passed between her parents. "Oh, I get it," she said, placing her hands firmly on her hips. "It's Ben, right? You think I'm getting too serious with Ben. You want to separate us so that he'll forget all about me. You never did like him, did you? And now you want to mess up my whole life just to get rid of him."

She turned and ran from the room, not wanting her parents to see her cry. She rushed into the kitchen and pushed open the screen door onto the porch. Then she flopped down onto the pillows of the wooden swing and lay there, rocking herself back and forth, watching the line of the golden, corn-filled horizon go up and down beyond the picket fence. The black-and-white cat walked down the porch and leaped up to join her.

Bonnie, the golden retriever, came to put her wet nose in Chrissy's face, and offered a consoling kiss.

Chrissy lay there, absentmindedly stroking Bonnie with one hand and the cat with the other. Images tumbled through her mind: a magical city, hills covered with tall buildings, wide blue waters spanned by great bridges. Even as she formed the picture of San Francisco in her mind, her heart leaped with excitement. But she forced that picture away and summoned new images: a battered red truck, hair the color of corn flopping across a pink forehead, and bright blue eyes smiling at the sight of her. She saw the familiar grin and heard the comforting voice call, "Come on now, girl, hop on up. Don't keep me waiting all day!" Then she imagined herself running from the house in response to impatient honking—but something was wrong with the picture. She was no longer dressed in her everyday blue jeans and checked shirt; she wore elegant city clothes and glided gracefully on heels three inches high. She could see Ben's puzzled face clearly as he wrinkled his forehead, shook his head, and exclaimed, "What have you been doing to yourself? You're all dressed up like a dog's dinner."

"No way," she said firmly to Bonnie and the cat. "I can't leave my home for a year. I already told them I couldn't even think of going away to college for a whole year. A strange high school would be ten times worse. And Ben. How could I leave Ben? He'd never understand why I'd want to leave Danbury. He'd sure enough find someone else."

"Hi, pumpkin," a soft voice behind her said. Chrissy started so that both Bonnie and the cat jumped, too.

She'd been so lost in the awful thought of losing Ben that she hadn't heard her mother come out through the screen door.

"I guessed I'd find you here," she said, perching on one end of the swing seat. "Do you mind if I join you?"

Chrissy shrugged her shoulders but didn't sit up. "But it's no use trying to make me change my mind," she warned. "I'd love to go to California, but not for a year. I can't understand what's gotten into you, wanting to send me away like that. I'd have thought you'd miss me, too." Her voice cracked at the end of the sentence, and she stared out at the vegetable garden, unable to look at her mother.

Her mother leaned over and ruffled her hair. "Of course we'll miss you, honey," she said fondly. "It will almost break my poor heart to be without you for that long. But you're thinking of this all wrong. We're honestly trying to do what we think is best for you. It's not fair to accuse us of planning some kind of punishment to take you away from Ben."

"Well, what else is it?" Chrissy asked mournfully. "I heard you telling Daddy just last night that you didn't want us getting too serious."

"But it's not only because of Ben that we want you to go away," her mother said gently. "I want you to go for my sake. I want you to have the chance I never had."

Chrissy turned and looked up at her mother's tired, lined face. "What do you mean?" she asked.

Her mother sighed and pushed back a wisp of hair that had escaped from the knot she always wore. "I'm going to tell you something I've never told anyone before," she said. "Not even your Dad." Chrissy propped herself up on one elbow and turned to face her mother. "I was just your age when my sister went away to college," she said dreamily. "Just sixteen. I remember it so clearly. Edith got a scholarship to the University of California in Berkeley. I remember feeling so envious as she packed her bags and went off on the bus. Well, that was the sixties, and Edith soon got herself mixed up in all the political stuff of that time—you know, demonstrations against the war in Vietnam. First, she got arrested a couple of times at sit-ins on the campus. Then she came home with this boy she said she wanted to marry. They both had long hair, right over their shoulders, and they were wearing long robes and flowers in their hair. You should have seen my parents' faces when they got off the bus! Your grandpa took one look at the boy and ordered him out of the house. There was an ugly quarrel, with everyone but me doing a lot of yelling. Your aunt Edith went with him and we never saw her again.

"After that my parents made it very clear that I was not going away to college. That was fine with me at the time. I didn't want to be part of the sort of life Edith was leading, and I didn't want my folks yelling at me the way they yelled at Edith. Besides, there was this boy I was dating from school, and we got married right after graduation."

She paused for a moment and stared off into the

distance, then she looked down at Chrissy with a little smile. "Oh, I've been happy myself. I can't say I'd want to change much about my life, but sometimes I still wonder—I wonder what I might have made of my life if I'd gone away and learned a few new ideas."

She reached across and put her hand gently on Chrissy's arm. "I want you to have that chance," she said. "I want you to see different places and different ways of life, so that if you do decide to marry and settle down here, you'll know you're doing the right thing, and you won't always wonder, the way I do."

Then she got up and walked quietly back into the house. After she had gone, Chrissy got up and called to Bonnie, who had wandered out into the yard. Then she started to walk. She walked past the dusty garden where her mother tried to coax roses to bloom every summer, along the track to the road, beside the fields of new corn, green and shoulder high, rustling like taffeta in the evening breeze. When she reached the road into town she kept walking. Kansas daisies bloomed here and there in the tall grass, and cows looked up from a meadow beyond the fence. As she crossed the railroad tracks, she looked carefully up and down, as she had been taught, and realized, with a start, that she was always a little disappointed when no big engine was approaching. She loved to watch the trains rush past, wondering who was on them and where they were going, following them with her eyes until they were specks of movement in the distance.

Maybe I do want to travel someday, she thought.

Maybe I do want to see the rest of the world. But I'm not ready yet.

She walked on. Ahead on the arrow-straight road, she could see the cluster of houses that made up Danbury, POP 355. She knew all those three hundred fifty-five people. Many of them were cousins or the cousins of cousins. Every inch of Danbury was familiar to her. Grandma Madden lived across from the high school, and uncle Homer ran the gas station. If she passed a cat in the street, it came to rub against her and she called it by name, if it had one. She even knew the name of every hog at the Meyers' farm next door. The thought of a city filled with thousands of people who didn't even recognize her face caused her to shiver.

"But it would be exciting, too," she whispered to herself, half-ashamed to be thinking it. A person could probably walk down a new street every day in San Francisco, shop in new stores, see a new face passing the house each time she looked out the window. *And it's not as if I'd be totally alone*, she thought. *I'd have family there. Aunt Edith seemed like a friendly person, and I'd have a cousin just my age. It would almost be like having the sister I've always wished for, ready made. We could gossip and listen to records together and go to movies.* A brand new thought struck her. In big cities, folks had hundreds of movies to choose from every day. And in California, the ocean was right there. Caroline was probably always going to beach parties, surfing and watching movie stars get discovered while they lay on the sand. So many experiences were only names to Chrissy so far.

As she reached the first houses of the town, a collection of buildings too small really to deserve that title, old Jed Guthrie shuffled down his front path to collect his evening paper. Five o'clock. When Chrissy came home late from school after cheerleading practice, she always passed Jed shuffling out to get his paper. He looked up as usual when he heard her footsteps.

"Evenin', Miss Chrissy," he said in his slow, deliberate voice. "Reckon it looks like a fine day tomorrow." Without waiting for Chrissy's reply, he turned and shuffled back toward his house.

Bonnie had run on ahead, obviously thinking they were heading for Grandma Madden's house. Chrissy whistled to her and she turned, her head to one side, waiting for her next command.

"Come on, Bonnie," Chrissy said. "Let's go home."

"I've never heard you complain about life in Danbury, old girl," Chrissy said as Bonnie came bounding toward her, stirring up clouds of dust in the dirt. As Chrissy turned to walk back down the road, she thought of the faraway look that appeared in her mother's eyes when she stood doing the dishes and listening to the radio in the evening. She stooped down and grabbed Bonnie around the neck, rubbing her cheek against the dog's warm fur. "I could always come home again if I really hated it, I guess," she said after a moment. Bonnie's answer was a sloppy lick on the face.

That evening Ben came for dinner, as he did several nights a week. No one mentioned San Francisco. Chrissy looked from one familiar face to the next; she took in the way her father's eyes crinkled at the sides when her middle brother, Will, told him a funny story, the way her little brother, Jimmy, stuck out his tongue in concentration as he tried to cut his pot roast, and the way her oldest brother, Tom, sat up tall so that he could catch a glimpse of himself in the speckled, gilt-framed mirror behind her father's head. They were all so dear—how could she ever leave them?

The setting sun coming in through the west window threw a warm light onto all their faces as well as the sturdy maple furniture that had been Grandma's and probably her parents' before that. Everything in the huge kitchen was friendly and familiar: the row of blue plates on the high shelf, the big grandfather clock in the corner, the roll-top desk where Chrissy's mother did the family accounts. She loved this home and couldn't imagine any other.

She looked across at Ben and caught his eye. He smiled at her. "Your ma bakes the best cornbread I've ever tasted," he said. "Only don't you go telling my mother that!"

"Why, thank you, Ben," Chrissy's mother said, blushing with pleasure.

"I hope you're teaching Chrissy to cook," Ben said, grinning across at her. "Those brownies she baked for the picnic last summer almost took my teeth out!"

"They did not, Ben Hatcher," Chrissy said angrily, rising, as usual, to his teasing. "Besides, I have other talents besides cooking."

Her brothers let out a chuckle at this.

"Name one?" Will demanded.

"I'm the best cheerleader on the squad," she said. "I got the best grade on the county-wide American history test this spring, and I won prizes with my rabbits at Four-H."

The boys chuckled loudly when Chrissy finished. "I reckon cheerleading will come in real useful some day," her brother Tom commented.

"Yeah, she can wave her pom-poms to round up the cattle," Will quipped.

"Nah, she can throw her brownies at them." Tom jumped and rubbed his side as if one of Chrissy's brownies had just caught him in the ribs.

Chrissy didn't say anything. Any other time she would have laughed with her brothers and started to hurl insults back at them. But in her present mood, the good-natured teasing was causing her to realize something clearly for the first time. The boys—even Ben—spoke as if being a farmer's wife were the only future she could expect. It didn't matter to them what she could do if she couldn't cook well enough to please their stomachs. She ate the rest of her meal silently, and listened to the conversation flow easily around her. Even the talk stayed within twenty-five miles of Danbury—the outbreak of swine fever over at King City, the Rogers' new harvester, the number of jars of strawberry jelly still left in the pantry.

When the boys had cleaned the last speck of crust from the peach pie tin, Chrissy got up to help her mother clear the table.

"You were awful quiet tonight," her mother said gently. "Were you doing some thinking?"

Chrissy nodded. "I've been thinking about what you said earlier. It's a pretty small world we live in. There's an awful lot of things I'll never see if I spend my entire life in Danbury. Maybe I should think of going to California."

After the dishes were dried, Chrissy and Ben walked out onto the back porch. It was a soft, warm night. Lightning bugs were winking in the blackness.

"Your aunt get back to California safely?" Ben asked as he closed the screen door behind them.

"I reckon so," Chrissy said. "Ma was going to call tonight."

Ben walked across and leaned on the porch rail, staring out into the blackness beyond. "I wonder what she thought of us?" he said easily. "I reckon she thought we were real backwards."

"She did not," Chrissy protested. "She seemed very nice."

"I heard her telling your ma she should get herself a microwave oven to save her time. She said everyone in San Francisco has one."

Chrissy hesitated. "Well, I suppose it would speed things up."

"Who needs things speeded up?" Ben asked. "That's the trouble with city folks. They never have any time. Remember that time I went to Chicago? I got pushed and shoved right into the traffic when I didn't cross the street soon enough. And everybody dressed up in their best clothes all the time, just like your aunt. No wonder they're in a hurry—they spend half the morning worrying about what to wear. I didn't see any blue jeans in downtown Chicago."

"I've never even seen a big city at all," Chrissy said slowly.

Ben snorted. "You have, too. You've been to Des Moines and Omaha, haven't you?"

"I know," Chrissy said. "But I mean a real city, one like Chicago where it's all houses packed close together and different kinds of people filling the sidewalks, and skyscrapers you can climb to the very top—then look out and still not see the end of it all."

"Why would you want to do that?" Ben asked, horrified. "Think of all that pollution."

Chrissy snorted. "Even Danbury's polluted. We have the hogs right next door here," she reminded him. "Besides, think of the movie houses and the big stores and the live theaters. You could see a different movie every night for a week!"

"You're welcome to it," Ben said. He continued to stare out into the blackness. Chrissy leaned down beside him at the rail and put her hand on his shoulder.

"Ben?" she said. "I might decide to go to a city. I might go spend some time with my aunt in California. They have a real good school there, and I have a cousin just my age I've never seen. . . ."

Ben didn't move or speak. He continued staring.

"My mom says it would be a wonderful chance for me," Chrissy went on. "And I guess it would be. I'd be seeing the ocean and skyscrapers and all the things I've dreamed of seeing one day . . . but . . ." Her voice faltered. He turned to look at her.

"But what?"

"But I don't want to leave you," she said, gazing up at him.

"I hope you don't want me to come to San Francisco with you," he said suspiciously.

Chrissy had to laugh. "No, I can't see you in San Francisco," she said gently. "But I just wanted you to know that leaving you would be the one thing holding me back."

"You go if that's what you want," Ben said flatly.

"I don't know what I really want," Chrissy said with a sigh. "That's the problem. If I could bundle up the farm and my family and you take them all with me to San Francisco, I'd go like a shot."

"Look, Chrissy, I'm not going to pretend I like this idea. But I know you well enough to know I'd be a fool to try and stop you," he said. "I think this is something where you've got to make up your mind for yourself."

Later that night Chrissy lay in bed, watching the moonlight shine through the branches of the big cottonwood tree. She tossed and turned, but sleep wouldn't come. Conflicting thoughts chased one another through her mind. She closed her eyes and tried to picture herself in downtown San Francisco, as elegantly dressed as Aunt Edith had been. It was scary, but it also sent a thrill of excitement through her. *Ben says I've got to make up my own mind, and he's right. Make up my own mind, make up my own mind.* How many times in her life had she been asked to make up her own mind about anything before? All her life, somebody else had decided for her. Or maybe there just hadn't been very many choices. For the first time, she held her future in her own hands.

It's not as if it's forever, she told herself. *I could come home on vacations. And if I really hated it, I'd just get right on the next plane home. What have I got to lose?*

Ben! I could lose Ben to another girl.

Next morning before the sun was fully up, Chrissy dressed and saddled up Posey, the old mare, and rode over to Ben's house. Ben was already up, as she knew he would be, coming out of the barn with a bucket of mash for the hens. His eyes lit up when he saw her in a way that almost melted her heart.

"You come to tell me you've made up your mind?" he asked hesitantly.

Chrissy slid from the mare's back. "I've been thinking about it all night, and I really think I should go," she said quickly, afraid she wouldn't be able to finish if she hesitated. "I'd write a lot and I'd be home on vacations and it's only until June."

Ben came across to her with giant strides. He put down the bucket and slipped his big hands around her waist.

"Chrissy," Ben said firmly, "go if you want to. You don't need me to say yes. Do what you want to do. I'll still be here when you come back."

"But will you still be here for me, Ben?" Chrissy asked. "I guess that's what I want to know. I can't really ask you to stick around, waiting for me, if I go off someplace, but I don't want to lose you."

"I'll stick around," he said. "You can be sure of that.

Just don't you go getting yourself all citified and come back here looking like your aunt!"

Chrissy wound her arms around his neck. "Of course I won't, dummy," she whispered. "Nothing can ever change the way I am or the way I feel about you."

"That's good," she whispered back, "because I like you just the way you are." Then he kissed her tenderly, holding her close for a long while.

Chrissy galloped Posey home at a pace that surprised the old mare and let herself in quietly through the screen door. "I guess you can call Aunt Edith now," she said to her mother, "and tell her to get the spare bed made up."

One

Caroline walked slowly up the hill, trailing a string bag of vegetables. She kept glancing across to the blue-and-white house on the right, even though she was pretending to be interested in the cracks on the sidewalk. It was the second time she had walked past the big Victorian house, but she hadn't yet got up enough nerve to go ring the doorbell. Her boyfriend, Alex, lived there, and she kept hoping that he would appear miraculously at his front door and just happen to notice her across the street.

What are you waiting for, you idiot! she scolded herself. *Just go over there and knock on his door. What's so hard about that? He is your boyfriend, after all. He'll be pleased to see you.*

But still she hung back. She knew that most of her friends wouldn't think twice about dropping in to visit their boyfriends, but Caroline just wasn't the sort of person who dropped in on a person unexpectedly, even if the person in question was her boyfriend. Besides, she and Alex hadn't been going together for very long. They had only really started dating toward the end of sophomore year. Then he had been away working as a camp counselor for most of the summer. She still felt uncomfortable when she phoned him and his mother answered.

She hadn't planned to visit Alex this morning, but she had been walking down his street on her way back from the Chinatown market where her family always did their vegetable shopping when she'd been overwhelmed by an impulse to see him. Ever since her mother had dropped the bombshell about her country cousin, Caroline had needed someone to talk to. Her oldest friend, Maria, was away for the summer, and Tracy and Justine were touring Europe, so Caroline had been on her own for quite a while.

She drew level again with Alex's house. Then, taking a deep breath, she crossed the street and rang the doorbell.

"Caroline! Just the person I wanted to see!" Alex greeted her with a huge smile.

"Really?" Caroline asked, flushing with pleasure and kicking herself mentally for agonizing over whether to ring the doorbell. Alex would have thought she looked like a fool if he'd seen her pacing the sidewalk.

"You bet," Alex said, bending forward to give her a quick kiss. "Come on in. You got here just in time. You're the only person I know who's neat enough to pack my backpack for me."

"Oh," Caroline said, her face falling. The trouble with Alex was that she never quite knew when he was teasing and wasn't secure enough yet with him and his crowd to laugh off the put-downs.

Alex turned back to her and read her face instantly. "You are a dope," he said gently. "Of course I want to see you. I want to see you anytime. Only right now I'm twice as happy because of all this stupid packing."

"You're going away again?" Caroline asked, following him down the hall toward his room. "You just got back from camp."

"This is vacation," Alex said in a dubious voice. "At least, it's supposed to be vacation. My father called from L.A. last night to tell me he set up this high-country backpacking trip for just the two of us."

"I didn't know your dad was outdoorsy like that," Caroline commented. Alex looked back at her and made a face. "He wasn't," he said. "But he's been into physical fitness ever since the divorce. It started with the health club and jogging, and now he's really flipped. He wants us to hike the Pacific Crest Trail."

"That doesn't sound too bad," Caroline ventured, but Alex made a tortured face.

"The Pacific Crest Trail goes over the mountains," he said. "Up one side and down the other as if they weren't there. Have you ever tried walking up a mountain with three tons on your back? He said he thought it would be fun to make a base camp and conquer some major peaks!" Alex laughed again. "I'm just hoping he's not in the shape he thinks he is and he wants to quit after the first day," he said. "Come see what he thinks I'm going to carry on my back."

He pushed open his bedroom door. They both stood in the doorway because further entry to the room was impossible. Every surface was covered with equipment. Clothing, rope, first-aid supplies, cooking gear, a sleeping bag, and ground sheets covered the floor. Alex laughed again and shook his head in despair.

"What the well-equipped backpacker needs for survival," he said.

Caroline's eyes still were taking in the clutter. "You're planning to take all this with you?" she asked. "On your back?"

Alex sighed. "My Dad dictated a list of supplies we'll need over the phone. I have a feeling it's not all going to go into one backpack."

"Alex, this is crazy," Caroline said, laughing for the first time. "There's no way one person can carry all this. How long are you planning to be away?"

Alex rolled his eyes toward the ceiling. "He thinks maybe three weeks. He says we should take enough for three weeks just in case we get snowed in on a peak or holed up in a storm. Doesn't that sound exciting?"

Caroline pointed at a huge mound of foil packets. "What are all these?" she asked.

"That's our food," Alex said, reaching to pick one from the top of the pile. "All freeze dried. Just add water. Look at this one—pancakes, eggs, and coffee all in one bag."

"Yuck!" Caroline shuddered. "It sounds disgusting."

"Yes, please think of me having to eat it when you're lounging in your nice warm bed and getting up to real breakfasts," Alex said. "Of course," he added, "You could always come along as the expedition cook, and then we wouldn't have to eat this stuff. I'm sure you'd just love to tramp up and down a few mountains with fifty pounds on your back."

Caroline tiptoed into the room and absently began poking at the packets of food. "Right now that doesn't sound too terrible," she said. "In fact, I think I might prefer it to what's in store for me next week."

"What?" Alex asked.

"I get to show my cousin around San Francisco," Caroline said with a sigh.

Alex looked puzzled. "Is that so bad?" he asked. "What's wrong with your cousin? I didn't even know you had any cousins."

"Neither did I," Caroline said. "I only discovered her existence when Mom went to my grandmother's funeral last week. It seems I have a whole family back in Iowa. My mother fought with them years ago about marrying my dad, and she hadn't been in touch with them since. Anyway, my mother went over there and saw her sister again and found out that Aunt Ingrid has four kids, one of them a girl exactly my age."

"So that should be fun for you, shouldn't it?" Alex asked.

Caroline was still fingering the packages. "I don't know, Alex," she said. "To tell you the truth, I'm kind of nervous."

"The rest of your family are vampires, or what?" Alex quipped. Caroline smiled. "Look, you're making a big deal out of a little thing, Cara. I had to make room for three steps when my dad got remarried. Lots of people do it. You'll survive."

"I'm sure she's really nice, Alex, and I do want to

meet her. In fact I'd love it if she were coming to stay for a couple of weeks. We'd have a great time, I'm sure."

"So how long is she coming for?"

"A whole year," Caroline muttered. "My mother, in a fit of generosity, invited her to share my room for a whole year!"

"Why don't you wait until she gets here before you decide it'll be so terrible? She might turn out to be a fun person. After all, if she's anything like you—"

"Mom says she looks a lot like me," Caroline began.

"That sounds like good news to me," Alex interrupted. "Another gorgeous girl for me to flirt with!"

"Alex!" Caroline said, glaring at him.

Alex chuckled. "What I was about to say is that if she's anything like you, she'll be very nice," he said hastily. "Relax, Cara. Try not to worry so much about things that may never happen."

"I do try," Caroline said. "But I can't help it, Alex. It's just the way I am. I lay awake last night imagining all sorts of terrible things—that she'd come tramping through my room with manure on her boots, and that she'd smell bad and eat like a pig."

Alex put a protective arm around her shoulder. "Like I said, Cara, try to relax. Your mother's met this girl, right? Do you think she'd invite someone like you're describing to share your home for a whole year?"

Caroline shrugged her shoulders. "I don't know. You know how my mother loves charity cases. Maybe she wants to do a *My Fair Lady* act on Chrissy and turn her into a young lady. I mean, even if she isn't as bad as I'm imagining, she'll still be straight from the farm. And I'll be the one who has to take her to school with me every day."

"So?" Alex asked, puzzled.

Caroline sighed impatiently. "Oh, Alex, be reasonable. How is a girl in overalls going to fit in with our friends?"

"You wear overalls sometimes," Alex suggested. "Admit it. I remember a yellow pair last year."

"But those weren't farm overalls, Alex," Caroline explained patiently. "Those were designer overalls."

"What's the difference, besides an expensive label on yours?"

"There's lots of difference," Caroline said.

Alex threw back his head and laughed. "I don't think I'll ever be able to understand what goes on in girls' heads," he said. "What does it matter what she wears?"

"It matters a lot, Alex," Caroline said, picking up a pair of thick woolen socks from his bed and playing with them as she spoke. "I just don't want to be laughed at because I've got a hick trailing around behind me. You wouldn't understand, because you get along with people so easily. Everyone likes you. Not me. The first two years of high school I hardly spoke to anyone. If a strange kid stopped and asked me something in the hall, I'd clam up with fright. Then I met all of you guys, and that was terrific for me. But you know what Justine and the others are like. They travel around the world and they know exactly what to say or eat or wear all the time. I don't want them to think I'm a weirdo in disguise because of my cousin."

"I think you've got it wrong, Cara," Alex said gently. "I really don't think things like designer labels matter so much to Justine or the rest of the crowd."

"I'm not saying they're snobby or shallow, Alex," Caroline said hastily. "They're not. But they're used to a pretty sophisticated life style, and I can't exactly see them letting something out of the *Beverly Hillbillies* tag along. I'm just beginning to feel like I fit in myself," she added, twisting one of his wool socks into a tight knot as she spoke. "I don't want to find myself on the outside again because of somebody else. You can understand that, can't you?"

Alex slipped his arm from her shoulder and gently caressed the back of her neck. "Sure I can," he said. "But I still think you're worrying about nothing. Wait and see what your cousin's like. Coming from a farm doesn't make her a hillbilly, you know."

Caroline laughed uneasily. "I'm sure she'll be just fine, really. It's just that . . ." She hesitated again, then nestled her head against Alex's shoulder. "It's the thought of any stranger coming into my life for a whole year."

"I was a stranger last May," Alex said, bending his face toward her tenderly.

Caroline gazed up at him. "But you weren't from the other side of the planet," she said.

"What do you really know about me?" Alex asked in a sinister voice. "For all you know, I could really be a creature from the planet Pluto, and when I peel off this human skin, I'm all green and slimy underneath." He pretended to unzip his throat.

Caroline laughed and flung her arms around his neck. "Oh, Alex," she said. "You're terrific."

"You're not so bad yourself," he whispered, suddenly serious as his arms tightened around her. "In fact, I think we make a great couple." His lips moved down to meet hers, and for a long moment they stood like that, their arms wrapped around each other.

"I—er—thought you only brought me here to do your packing," Caroline said shakily when they finally broke apart.

Alex groaned and looked in despair around the room. "Yeah, I suppose we'd better get on with it. You can help me decide what to take and what not to. Then if I'm missing something vital when I'm clinging by my fingertips to the edge of some cliff, I can blame you."

"You say the sweetest things," Caroline said, starting to sift through the piles of clothing. "Here, pass me one of those sweaters. You don't need five sweaters. Talk about girls being vain about their clothing!"

"You mean I can't take the big black-and-white one?" Alex asked in a hurt voice.

"Only if you want no spare socks and not enough food."

"You're mean. If I'm eaten by bears who are offended by my tasteless wardrobe, I'll blame you," he quipped. "I don't think I'll take you out tonight for a farewell pizza after all. I'll wait and take out your cute cousin instead!"

"Tonight?" Caroline asked. She frowned. "I couldn't come tonight anyway."

Alex's face fell. "Don't tell me it's the dreaded ballet again? I thought ballet school shut down for the summer."

"It does," Caroline said. "But tonight and tomorrow night are tryouts for the performing company. I told you about it, didn't I? They take the twelve best students into the company each year, and those students get to dance in real ballets."

"And you want to get into it?" he asked.

"My folks think it would be a wonderful chance," Caroline said hesitantly.

"And you?" Alex asked. "Do you think it would be a great idea?"

Caroline hesitated. "Sometimes I do," she said. "But I'm not sure whether I'm good enough yet. Sometimes I'm scared of all the extra work and extra pressure it will mean, but at least I'll be able to know if I'm cut out to be a ballerina, won't I?"

"I suppose I'll be seeing even less of you," Alex said, punching T-shirts into one of the side pockets of his pack without looking at her. "I'll have to make an appointment to talk to you between four and five on November first."

Caroline looked at him tenderly.

"Oh, Alex, it won't be that bad," she said. "I'll make time. You mean a lot to me, too. How about if we go out for an early pizza tonight? My tryouts don't start until six."

"I guess," Alex said. "We could fit in an early pizza around five."

"Terrific," Caroline said. "You'll have to excuse me if I just eat a salad because I won't be able to jêté if I eat pizza, but I can't let you go out into the wilds without saying good-bye first."

"That's okay," Alex said, grinning at her. "I plan to eat enough pizza for both of us. Who knows when I'll get real food again?"

Two

"Now, Caroline," Caroline's mother said, drawing her aside, "I want to remind you of a few things before Chrissy actually arrives."

They were waiting together for Chrissy at San Francisco International Airport, at the edge of the security area. Caroline's father had wandered into the airport bookstore, leaving Caroline and her mother alone.

"I know," Caroline said with a little sigh. "I've got to be nice to Chrissy. I know that, Mother. Don't worry, I'm going to try very hard."

"I'm sure you will, honey," her mother said. "But I wanted to stress a couple of things to you, so that you can help Chrissy settle in here. You see, she's never been away from home before, so she's going to feel very strange to begin with. It will be a tremendous shock to come from a farm to the middle of a city. You'll have to take care of her. She'll probably be scared to go out alone for a while."

Caroline digested this information, trying to imagine what it would be like to see a city for the first time. She had never lived anywhere else. "I guess dodging in and out of traffic could be frightening," she agreed. "And finding your way around . . ."

"And it won't be just the city that is frightening for her," Caroline's mother continued. "She will be very homesick, I'm sure. She's never left her family before. So it's up to all of us to make her feel at home here."

For the first time, Caroline realized that to come to San Francisco, Chrissy had to leave behind her family and friends and hometown. She had thought only that anybody would be thrilled to come to California. Now she considered the idea that Chrissy would be scared and homesick. It only added weight to the load of responsibility Carrie had been handed. Not only was she to share her living space, her friends, and her school with a stranger, but it would be up to her to make sure that stranger wasn't scared or homesick. Suddenly she felt overwhelmed by her new, entirely unwanted, burden. The sinking feeling that she recognized from exam week and ballet recitals settled soundly in her stomach. The worries that had come and gone over the past few days of frantic preparation returned to the front of Caroline's mind. As she had emptied half her drawers and closet space for Chrissy, as she had rearranged her collection of china animals to make room for Chrissy on the shelves, as she had given up her view of the San Francisco Bay to fit in the extra bed, worries had flapped around inside her head. What if she and

Chrissy took one look at each other and hated each other's guts? What would they talk about every morning and every evening for a year? What if Chrissy snored at night, or walked in her sleep, or smelled like a barn?

"I know she's a relative," Caroline thought as she stared down the hallway. "But that doesn't necessarily mean we have anything in common. Why doesn't she hurry up and get here and end this misery?"

Another plane had landed and was dumping its passengers into the hall. Husbands and wives, parents and children, old friends ran toward one another to hug and kiss. Lone travelers stood looking for a friendly face, confused by the strange airport. Caroline recalled the excitement of landing in a new place for the first time. Of course, there were always the same old boring formalities to endure: endless lines to show passports, long waits for baggage to arrive from the plane, more waiting to have it examined by unsmiling customs officials. But the formalities were always bearable because of what lay beyond the customs halls: quaint, centuries-old towns of stone buildings or skyscraping palm trees or rain-drenched London streets—and always thousands of new faces teeming by, speaking in exotic, incomprehensible tones.

"I don't think I like being on the receiving end of traveling so much," Caroline said to her mother. "I wish *we* were going somewhere."

"You have been very lucky and done a lot of traveling for a girl of your age."

"Except for this summer," Caroline said, looking away across the airport.

"Don't let's go into that again, Caroline," her mother said sharply. "We are not millionaires. You can't just go running off to Europe every time you feel like it."

"But all my friends went," Caroline said. "I was the only one who had to sit home all summer."

"Next summer you'll be old enough to earn your own money to travel—think of it."

Caroline wrinkled her nose, something she often did when she was digesting information. "With my luck I'll probably have extra dance classes all next summer," she said.

"You make it sound as if ballet were a punishment," her mother commented.

"It feels that way sometimes. Sometimes I feel like the only freak among all my friends. I never seem to have time for them because of ballet."

"What about the performing company?" her mother asked. "You were so excited when you heard you'd got in."

Caroline nodded. "I know. I am excited. I didn't think I'd make it for a minute. Everyone else seemed so much better, and I messed up on so many things during tryouts. I still can't believe I got in."

"I wasn't surprised at all," her mother said. "I knew when you were five years old and had your first ballet lesson that you'd be a star one day."

Caroline laughed. "Mothers are always prejudiced," she said. "They all think their children are going to wind up as stars of something."

"Wouldn't you like to be a star?" her mother asked.

Caroline kicked at a candy wrapper that lay by her feet. "I don't know," she said hesitantly. "I don't know what I want. That's the problem. All those other girls at ballet school seem so dedicated. I'm not sure I'm ready to give up the rest of my life for ballet. I want my friends, too. I want to be able to go out for pizza."

Her mother gave her a smile of reassurance. "I understand," she said. "But it will be all worth it in the end when you get accepted into a major company. You'll be able to—" She broke off as the loud noise of approaching jet engines filled the terminal. "I think this must be Chrissy's plane now," she said. "Now please don't forget, Caroline. You're used to traveling. I doubt Chrissy has ever been out of Iowa. I know she's never been on a plane. She'll probably be terrified, poor little thing."

The huge white plane blocked the view from the windows beside a rear gate as Chrissy's plane pulled toward the terminal. Again a picture took shape in Caroline's mind. A girl with a gingham skirt and hair in braids—was it Dorothy, from *The Wizard of Oz?*—clung, terrified, to a mortified Caroline.

People began to come through the gate—businessmen in dark suits hurried past to catch taxis, mothers chased after small children, chic young women with briefcases clicked past on high heels, but there was no sign of the gingham skirt or the braids.

"Are you sure she's on the plane?" Caroline asked. "Maybe she chickened out at the last moment."

"She's on it," her mother said calmly. "I expect she's hanging back because she's not sure of what to do. I wish they'd let us go in and get her, poor little thing."

At that moment, two flight attendants emerged from the jetway. They were both laughing and talking to a tall beautiful girl with long, loose white-blond hair. She wore brand new blue jeans, high-heeled gray boots, a denim jacket, and a bright red bandana tied around her neck. Her high laugh floated down the hall toward Caroline and her mother.

"That was just great," she was saying. "I loved every minute of it!"

As Chrissy entered the corridor, she turned toward Caroline and her mother, now nearly alone beyond the security gate. Then she uttered a scream of delight that made some of the more nervous travelers actually drop their bags. "Aunt Edith!' she cried as she started running toward them, scattering passengers on either side of her. Caroline could feel her cheeks reddening. "I'm so glad to see you, Aunt Edith!" she called. "I've got so much to tell you! You can't believe what fun I've had. They give you free meals and sodas whenever you ask for them, and I got taken up to meet the pilot and—"

A gray-haired man with a silk scarf around his neck and an elegant leather bag in one hand had tapped Chrissy on the shoulder.

"Have a good time in San Francisco, Chrissy," he said, giving her a warm smile. "I enjoyed talking to you a lot."

Chrissy turned back to her aunt. "That was the man in the seat next to me. He helped me buckle myself in and told me what all the buildings were when we flew over the city—"

"Bye, Chrissy," one of the flight attendants called as he passed. "Enjoy your stay here."

"I will," Chrissy called back. "See you next time I go home, maybe!"

"Everyone was so friendly," she said, with a broad smile. "Flying is fun. They even showed a movie . . ." Chrissy's gaze moved across to Caroline, and her eyes lit up even brighter, as if someone had turned up the electricity behind them.

"You must be Caroline!" she exclaimed. "You don't know how much I've been waiting to meet you. It's like getting a ready-made sister. When you've got three brothers, sometimes all you want is another girl to talk to." She flung her arms around Caroline and hugged her hard.

Caroline hugged Chrissy lightly, a little embarrassed by this public scene. "I'm glad you enjoyed your first flight so much," she said. "Mom thought you might be scared." She shot her mother a look over Chrissy's shoulder. So much for the terrified, shy country bumpkin!

Chrissy released Caroline and grinned at her. "I guess I was a little scared at first," she said. "I guess I'm still a little scared. That's why I'm talking so much. I always get noisy when I lose my wits."

Caroline looked at her cousin with admiration. She couldn't imagine confessing her fears to a stranger. Fright turned her shy around new people, and even though she knew some people mistook her shyness for snobbishness, she never could have explained herself.

"Well, you don't have to feel scared anymore," she heard herself saying to Chrissy. "You're going to have a good time. There's so much to do in the city, and you'll really like Maxwell High."

Chrissy slipped her arm through Caroline's. "I can't wait," she said. "Ma told me I'd get to pick all my classes. At my school, everyone picked from two electives—shop for boys and home ec for girls!"

"*Mon Dieu,*" Caroline said with a laugh. "They wouldn't try such a sexist thing here. The students would all protest."

"Students never complain at my school," Chrissy said. "They still run it the old-fashioned way. The teachers make the rules, and the students obey them. Sometimes they make you feel like students are a real pain to have around—the school would run smoothly if they could only get rid of the kids."

Caroline laughed again. "Then Maxwell will be an eye-opener for you," she said. "The students are very aware of everything. They have protests about nuclear weapons, toxic waste, city planning. Last year even I got involved in a committee to preserve a row of gingerbread houses."

Chrissy eyed Caroline with disbelief. "You're putting me on," she said.

"No, honestly," Caroline said.

Chrissy's lips twitched into a smile. "Gingerbread houses?" she asked. "And I bet you want me to believe that the wicked witch lives in San Francisco, too."

Caroline smiled. "Oh no, I didn't mean real gingerbread. In the city we have a lot of very ornate, carved wood houses with turrets and porches—totally impractical but very pretty. We call them gingerbread. They wanted to pull down a whole row to put in a high rise. I started a petition at school, and we saved them."

"Hey, good for you," Chrissy said, beaming at her

cousin. "You're a fighter like me. I guess it must run in the family."

"I'm not usually a fighter," Caroline confessed. "I don't like pushing myself forward, but I'm really glad I did something about the houses. For one thing, I met a lot of really neat people at school. And I even met my boyfriend that way."

"Oh, you have a boyfriend. Is he cute?" Chrissy demanded.

Caroline felt herself flushing slightly. "I guess so," she ventured.

"Tall, dark, and handsome?"

Caroline nodded hesitantly. Her cheeks turned one stage redder.

"I knew it," Chrissy said. "I can just picture you with a tall, dark, and handsome boyfriend. Tell me all about him!"

Caroline wriggled her toes inside her sneakers in embarrassment. She had only met this person five minutes earlier, yet she was already asking nosy, personal questions about Caroline's entire life! "You'll meet him soon," she said. "Then you can judge for yourself."

"I just hope he's not so super cute that I fall madly in love with him," Chrissy said. Caroline had to glance at her to make sure she was teasing. Chrissy saw Caroline's glance and grinned.

"Just kidding," she said. "You don't have to worry about me at all. I have a boyfriend back home. Did your mom tell you all about him? His name's Ben. The first thing you notice about him are the blond bangs he's forever pushing off his forehead. The second thing you notice is that you can almost always find him behind the wheel of this old red truck his daddy gave him. He's really fine. I didn't want to leave him, but somehow they talked me into it." She was still smiling, but the light in her eyes had dimmed a little bit.

Caroline remembered what her mother had said about Chrissy and her boyfriend getting too serious and said nothing more.

As the girls talked, they had walked down to the baggage-claim area on the lower level of the airport ahead of Caroline's mother and father. At the sight of the wide black conveyor belt that lurched into action on its steel frame just as the girls arrived, Chrissy let out a yelp that Caroline thought might have permanently deafened her.

"Holy mazoley!" Chrissy exclaimed. "We can ride around while we're waiting for the bags!"

"Chrissy!" Caroline whispered, grabbing at her cousin's arm just before Chrissy could seat herself on the conveyor belt. "People will think you are weird."

"Sorry," Chrissy said with a sheepish grin. "I was just joking. Didn't mean to scare you. I guess I have too much energy after sitting on a plane all day."

Caroline positioned herself behind a pillar a few steps away from her parents and Chrissy to wait for the bags. She could feel her cheeks burning. She felt sure half the people in the baggage area were staring at her, assuming she was part of a set of newly arrived weirdos. *How am I going to survive a whole year with this girl if we can't even get safely out of an airport?* she thought, panic rising in her. She'd live in a constant state of embarrassment.

It seemed to take forever until Chrissy's battered old

suitcases appeared. "Here they are! This one's mine!" Chrissy sang out happily, pulling an old expandable suitcase, tied up with string, from among the designer sets. "This is the same bag my dad carried on his honeymoon. Isn't that something?"

Caroline rushed to help her put it on a skycap's cart as quickly as possible.

At last all of Chrissy's bags had been collected and loaded; and Chrissy, Caroline, and her parents were in the car, headed toward downtown San Francisco.

"For Pete's sake, I can't get over all this traffic," Chrissy exclaimed as they joined the freeway. "How do you drive in traffic like this?"

"This is light," Caroline's father said with a chuckle from the front seat. "You should see what rush hour looks like."

"Do you drive in this mess?" Chrissy asked Caroline.

"Not yet," Caroline said. "I haven't had a chance to sign up for driver's ed."

"You don't really need to drive in the city. Buses go everywhere. And it's nearly impossible to find parking spaces anyway," Caroline's mother said. "Do you drive yet, Chrissy?"

"Only tractors and things," Chrissy said. "Ben lets me drive his truck when no one's looking, but I don't have a license yet."

"That's one good thing," Caroline's father said dryly from the front seat. "At least my car is safe from two teenage drivers!"

"Oh, Daddy," Caroline said. "You are so prejudiced. I am going to be a great driver when I learn."

"I just hope I don't have to be the one who teaches you the hill start." Her father chuckled. "You'd be in the bay before you got into gear."

"We live on a hill," Caroline commented to her cousin. "You have to be very careful to curb your wheels right when you park, or the car might run away. The police come and give tickets all the time for cars without their wheels curbed the right way."

"I can't imagine city streets going up and down hills," Chrissy said dreamily. "Back home the cities are in flat blocks." She paused and giggled. "But then they only go about four blocks in either direction. I don't suppose they really count as cities at all."

The freeway swung over a gentle hill, and the city was before them, tall glass buildings reflecting the late-evening sun. On one side was the blue water of San Francisco Bay, spanned by its long bridge to Oakland.

"Oh, wow," was all Chrissy managed to say. She perched on the edge of her seat, as if not wanting to miss a thing. She said "Oh, wow," several more times before the car arrived at the city center. Then she silently craned her neck to peer up at the tall buildings.

"I just can't believe it," she finally said. "Do they sway much in the wind?"

"They sway in earthquakes," Caroline's father said.

"Oh, wow," Chrissy said again, but this time fear, rather than excitement, colored her words.

"Don't scare her like that, Richard," Caroline's mother said firmly. "Contrary to popular belief, Chrissy, this city does not sway every ten minutes. I've lived here for more than twenty years now, and I've only felt an earthquake once. And it only rattled the china. In fact, if I remember correctly, the china used to rattle much more back in Iowa during a big thunderstorm."

"It does," Chrissy agreed. "And they had a twister come through about twenty miles from us last year."

"I'd rather face an earthquake than a tornado," Caroline said, shuddering.

"And I'd rather face neither," her father said. "This is Union Square, Chrissy. All the expensive stores are around here."

"I can't wait to go shopping," Chrissy said. "Window shopping, I mean. I don't suppose I could afford a thing in stores like these."

"You wouldn't want to afford a thing in these stores," Caroline said. "They're all full of old-woman clothes. There are some really funky boutiques I can take you to if you want to go shopping."

"Yes, Chrissy," Caroline's father said solemnly, "she spends a fortune to come back with clothes that look as if someone had been wearing them for ten years."

"I do not, Daddy. They are in style this year. Nobody wears jeans that look new anymore." She broke off quickly when she realized that Chrissy's jeans did look brand-new. "That reminds me," she said quickly, "will you lend me your double-breasted black jacket for that concert on Saturday?"

"My jacket?" her father asked. "Why would you want a man's sportscoat in the middle of summer? Are we in for a sudden cold spell?"

"No, Daddy. It's in style right now to wear big jackets," Caroline said, lifting her eyes toward Chrissy. "Is the baggy look in in Iowa?"

"I don't think so." Chrissy hesitated. "If anyone wore her Dad's jacket, everyone else would think she was too poor to get a new coat."

"Well, don't worry, Chrissy," Caroline's mother said, turning to look at the girls. "Next week baggy will be out and the girls will be wearing paper mini-skirts or spray-painting themselves green."

"Mother, you said yourself it was good to have us express ourselves," Caroline commented. It hurt for her mother to put her down in front of a virtual stranger. Any other time her mother was as interested as Caroline in the latest fashions. Now she was talking as if Caroline were silly and she and Chrissy were above it all. *I suppose she's only doing that to make Chrissy feel at ease*, Caroline decided. *But she might realize that I've got feelings, too.*

The car left downtown behind and began to climb a long, steep hill. A cable car passed them on its way down, bell clanging wildly. Chrissy stared in delight at the people hanging off the side.

"Can we do that one day?" she asked. "I can't wait to run up and down these hills!"

"You'll get tired of that fast," Caroline said. "Wait until you have to walk up our hill coming from school every day. It loses its thrill, I can tell you."

"Well, right now I can't wait," Chrissy said. "I'll probably wake everybody up at dawn tomorrow and drag you all out to explore the city!"

"You don't really get up at dawn, do you?" Caroline asked.

"Gosh, no," Chrissy said, laughing. "I'm a real late

sleeper. They have to drag me out of bed at six-thirty. My dad is always up by five."

"We're lucky to see Caroline before ten," Mr. Kirby commented.

"I stay up later than they do on farms," Caroline said. Why were her own parents making her feel so defensive?

The car had reached the top of the hill and began to descend the other side. "There's the Golden Gate Bridge!" Chrissy yelled. "And Alcatraz. It's all where it should be, just like in pictures and movies."

"And that's Fishermen's Wharf down below," Caroline pointed out. "I'll take you down there tomorrow, if you like."

"Oh, wow," Chrissy said again. "So many exciting things to do. It all looks wonderful. I am so glad I came."

"We're glad you came, too, dear," Mrs. Kirby said warmly. "And I've got a good idea, Richard. Why don't we take Chrissy out for dinner down at the Wharf, since it's her first night here?"

"Meaning that we have nothing to eat in the house again?" he asked with a chuckle.

"Oh no, please," Chrissy said hastily. "You don't have to take me out to eat. Golly, I'd be embarrassed if you did all that for me. I'm not used to fancy restaurants and things, and I already got lunch on the plane."

"But, Chrissy, we eat out a couple of times a week," Caroline explained, trying not to laugh. "It's no biggie for us. Dad hates to cook, and Mom doesn't have time."

"It's not exactly true that I hate to cook," her father cut in.

"But we're not exactly wild about your cooking," Caroline quipped back. "So since we don't want to poison Chrissy her first night here, let's go down to the Wharf. Good idea."

"I don't believe all this is happening to me," Chrissy said as the car pulled to a halt beside a tall, white three-story wooden house. "Everything's too good to be true."

Caroline watched as Chrissy climbed out and stared in wonder at the house, taking in its curved wooden turret on one corner, its steep steps, and its carved roof edges. Then she looked across the bay to where the lights of Sausalito were just beginning to twinkle.

"Is this your house?" she said, still staring. "It's huge!"

"We don't live in all of it," Caroline's mother said. "It's divided into apartments. We have the third floor. That's our little balcony over in the corner."

"It's beautiful," Chrissy sighed. "And the view is beautiful. *Everything's* just so beautiful. I feel like I'm in a dreamworld!"

Caroline was surprised to discover how Chrissy's reaction touched her. She had traveled with her parents from the time she was born, and she had been to places all around the world. She took her freedom to go anywhere for granted, so she hadn't even felt as excited as Chrissy did now even when she saw the Eiffel Tower for the first time. Now Chrissy made her see her own city through new eyes. It might just be fun to explore the Golden Gate Bridge and the park and Chinatown with her cousin. It would even be fun just to eat out with her.

Chrissy was standing on the sidewalk, gazing toward the water again, her eyes shining, her golden hair swept back by the breeze.

She's not at all how I imagined her, Caroline thought as she helped unload bags from the trunk. *She certainly doesn't look like a country bumpkin, and she's not the shy and scared little thing Mom predicted she would be. Everything will be just fine, and we'll have a great year together . . . I hope!*

Three

Caroline opened her eyes. It was dark in her room and she lay still for a moment, her heart beating fast, wondering what had woken her. Had she only dreamed of a roomful of mice, all scrabbling around her bed? She peered cautiously at the floor. Something really was moving across the rug. With a little yelp of horror she sat up.

The crawling thing skittered back, and Caroline saw it more clearly. It might have been a snake. Caroline winced to focus her sleepy eyes. Then she sighed in exasperation. It was only a snake if snakes ended in five fingers and wore frilly flannel nightgowns. But why was Chrissy slithering around the bedroom floor in the middle of the night?

Chrissy, crouching between the room's two beds,

dropped her extended arm to her side. She wore a guilty expression.

"Mama Mia, Chrissy, what are you doing?" Caroline asked, still half-scared and half-asleep.

"Oh, sorry. Did I wake you?" Chrissy said. "I was trying real hard not to, only I think my toothbrush holder rolled under your bed."

"But what do you want your toothbrush holder for in the middle of the night?" Caroline demanded.

"It's not the middle of the night. It's morning. I was going to the bathroom to take my shower before the rest of you got up."

"But it's still dark, Chrissy. What time is it?"

"By Iowa time it's around eight. I've never slept this late in my life!" Chrissy said.

"And what is it California time?" Caroline asked wearily.

"Nearly six. I guess that's a little early for you all, seeing that it's vacation, isn't it?"

"You might say that," Caroline said.

"I'm sorry," Chrissy said. "I'll just tiptoe to the bathroom, and you can go back to sleep again.

Caroline lay back and closed her eyes. Six o'clock on a summer morning! It was too much for any civilized person to bear. She pulled the covers up over her head.

Caroline was just drifting back into a comfortable sleep when she heard an agonized yell coming from the bathroom. She leaped out of bed and rushed across the hall.

"Chrissy? Are you okay?"

"Just soaked to my skin and scared out of my wits," Chrissy answered. "I decided to have a nice long tub bath instead of a shower, so I leaned over to turn on the faucets and put the stopper down and—whoosh—the water came out of the shower right onto the back of my neck."

"Oh, I'm sorry," Caroline said, laughing in spite of herself. "We usually take showers, so we leave the little button up all the time. I should have warned you."

"Well, at least I'm wet now," Chrissy said. "I'd better get the rest of me showered as fast as I can. It's pretty cold here in the mornings. I thought California would be baking hot."

"Not San Francisco," Caroline said. "It can be freezing in summer when the fog is in."

"I can't wait to see it all," Chrissy said. "Can we go around the city today? I want to ride on a cable car and go to all the expensive stores and walk along Fisherman's Wharf and see the ocean—"

"Not all in one day, I hope," Caroline said, laughing.

"As much as possible in one day," Chrissy said. "Can we get started after breakfast?"

"Sure. I guess," Caroline said, thinking wistfully of her warm bed.

"But you go back and sleep for a while more," Chrissy said. "I know I disturbed you, but I'm fine now. I can take my shower and dry my hair and you can get another hour of sleep. What time is breakfast?"

"No particular time," Caroline said. "We just fix ourselves something when we feel hungry. What do you usually like to eat for breakfast?"

"Oh, just any old thing. Nothing fancy," Chrissy

said. "A couple of eggs with some bacon and biscuits will do just fine."

Caroline's eyes opened very wide. "I suppose you must have more of an appetite working on a farm," she said. "I can usually just about manage a bowl of cereal or some fruit."

"My heavens, I'd die from starvation," Chrissy exclaimed. "You get used to a big breakfast when you have to walk a couple of miles to school in the morning. I'd never make it on fruit!"

"You finish your shower. I'll start cooking you some breakfast," Caroline said with a resigned sigh. She walked back to her room, slipped on her robe, and staggered to the kitchen. The clock on the wall said ten after six.

Is the rest of the vacation going to be like this? Caroline wondered, *or is she only getting up at this hour because her body clock is upset? I don't know if I can survive being woken at six every morning!*

Yawning as she dropped the fat strips of meat onto the pan, Caroline broke a couple of eggs into a skillet. Chrissy arrived just as the eggs finished cooking. She was wide awake and dressed, and Caroline noticed how really pretty she was. She had tied back her long blond hair into a pony tail and was wearing a red-and-white-checked shirt with a full white skirt. Her skin had a glow to it that must have come from living in the fresh air and eating lots of fresh farm food.

"Here," Caroline said, pushing the plate of food in front of Chrissy at the table.

"What about yours?" Chrissy asked. "Aren't you going to have breakfast, too?"

"Er, no thanks," Caroline said. "I think I'll go take a shower and see if I can wake myself up, then I'll grab a peach."

"You'll waste clean away," Chrissy warned. "And I have a feeling you are going to need plenty of energy today, because I am raring to explore!"

She walked over to the window. "I can't wait to see the view by daylight," she said. "It was almost dark when we got here last night." She drew back the drapes dramatically then let out a yell.

"What's wrong now?" Caroline asked, halfway down the hall to the shower.

"The city's gone!" Chrissy wailed. "There's nothing there outside!"

Caroline laughed. "That's just the good old San Francisco fog," she said. "Don't worry. It will burn off by around midday."

"We have fogs at home," Chrissy said, staring in wonder at the white blanket below them. "But nothing like this. It looks just like the clouds under the plane yesterday. It's like living on top of the world."

"You'd better stop gazing and eat your eggs," Caroline said. "They'll get cold in a minute."

Caroline made her way back wearily to her room, took her shower, and was about to climb into the oversized baggy shorts and safari top that had been her favorite uniform all summer. Then she remembered that Chrissy had decided to dress up for her day in the city. Caroline didn't want Chrissy to think she'd done the wrong thing, so she pulled on a huge red sweat shirt, hand painted with bright black squiggles, and black cotton stretch pants beneath it.

Caroline was proud of the sweater. She had agonized for days over the amount of money it cost; she could have bought a complete outfit for the same price. But she finally had gone into the boutique and bought it. All the compliments she got at school made her glad that she had decided to be daring for once. But as she appeared in the kitchen doorway to ask Chrissy if she was ready to go, Caroline could tell at once that Chrissy was not at all impressed.

"Oh gee," Chrissy said, looking a little embarrassed, "Did I get too dressed up? Should I go change into some old clothes?"

Caroline swallowed back the desire to tell her cousin that the sweat shirt had been designed by a man who designed clothes for rock stars and that stretch pants were what you wore with it. After all, how could somebody who lived out in the boonies possibly know what was fashionable? *It's just going to take some time to educate her,* Caroline decided. She gave Chrissy an encouraging smile. "That's okay. You look fine," she said. "Anything goes in this city."

"Okay. Let's go," Chrissy sang out, loudly enough, Caroline was sure, to wake her parents and the neighbors on the floor above. "I can't wait another second! This is the most exciting moment in my whole life, next to the time one of the mares had twins."

Caroline took a look at Chrissy's face. She was like a kindergartner on her way to a birthday party. Her eyes actually glowed with excitement. Caroline couldn't help feeling a little friendlier toward her cousin. It would be fun to show San Francisco to someone as enthusiastic as Chrissy. Caroline thought of the warm glow she felt when she knew she had chosen just the perfect present for one of her friends and anticipated how excited the friend would be when she opened it. That warm glow crept through her as she imagined Chrissy's first ride on a cable car or her first look over the water to Alcatraz or the lights of the town of Sausalito.

"We'll see how tough you farm people really are," she said, laughing as she opened the door for Chrissy. "Let's see if you can stand up to the grand tour!"

The city streets were full of life. Men and women in suits hurried to work, their briefcases clutched under their arms. Many joggers were out, dressed in bright warm-up suits with sweat bands around their heads, weights in their hands, and radios clipped at their waists.

"Is there some sort of race on today?" Chrissy asked.

"Race? No," Caroline answered, puzzled.

"Then where are all these people running to?" Chrissy wanted to know.

"They're jogging," Caroline said.

"All of them?" Chrissy asked. "Back home, about the only people who run around like that are the cross-country team and George Adams, who always was a little weird."

"People here think it's important to stay in shape," Caroline suggested.

Chrissy let out a high giggle. "That's funny," she said. "I'll have to write home about this. My folks would think it was real strange that people need to run up and down hills just to get exercise. When we have free time, we rest."

As they reached the street corner, a cable car was

inching its way up the hill toward them, its bell clanging at each cross street. Chrissy's eyes lit up.

"Would you like to ride one into town?" Caroline asked.

"Would I ever," Chrissy exclaimed. "I've dreamed about doing this. I've seen them on so many movies."

"Come on, then, let's go," Caroline said, putting her arms on her cousin's shoulder and propelling her toward the stop. The cable car pulled up, and several people climbed on ahead of Chrissy and Caroline. "Oh great, I get to hang on to the outside," Chrissy said with a giggle. "I've seen that in the movies, too." She stood on the step, grabbing onto a pole.

"Hey, this is fun!" she called, leaning out so that her silken hair blew back in the breeze. The car reached the top of the hill and began its descent of the other side.

"I love this," Chrissy called. "I'm going to ride one of these every single day and hang out the side . . . *Ooooo!*"

The cable car tracks turned a sharp corner. Chrissy, caught unaware, was swung out wide, hanging onto the pole by her fingertips. A dozen hands reached out to grab her and pull her in again.

"Gee, I'm sorry," she said to the people who had saved her. "I had no idea they went around corners so fast. I've never ridden a cable car before. This is my first day in San Francisco. Just yesterday, I was back in Iowa. Everything here is so exciting. . . ."

Caroline couldn't concentrate on what Chrissy was saying. Her heart had skipped a beat when she saw Chrissy go flying out around the corner. Now she cringed in embarrassment as she heard Chrissy telling her life story to a crowd of strangers. *She's got to learn that you just don't speak to strange people in the city,* Caroline thought.

"What nice people there are here," Chrissy commented as they climbed off the cable car in Union Square. "Did you know that the brakeman has a cousin who lives in Iowa? Imagine that!"

They walked through the early-morning crowds around the big square. Caroline shook her head as Chrissy went on about the cable car. *I won't be able to let her out of my sight ever if she's going to fall off public transportation and talk to every smiling person around her,* she thought.

Will you relax about this? she lectured herself as they crossed a busy intersection and Chrissy arrived at the other side like any normal pedestrian. *Give the girl a break. It's her first day in the city. She's excited; she's also jet-lagged. She can't learn everything at once. She'll be fine once she's settled in. Won't she?*

Caroline's thoughts were interrupted by Chrissy racing off toward a row of street vendors. Most of them were just opening up their stands and putting out their jewelry and toys for display.

"It's like the state fair," she commented. "What fun! I've got to buy one of those darling wind-up monkeys and that puppy that barks. Look at that soldier with the drum, Caroline! Isn't he cute?"

Caroline had a brief vision of her room full of monkeys clapping cymbals, dogs yapping, and birds flapping their wings. "I'll tell you what," she said. "Let's go get a croissant at the French bakery."

"See, I told you you should have eaten a good breakfast," Chrissy said. "Now you're hungry and you've got to spend money."

"But I like eating a croissant when I'm out," Caroline said. "We usually stop by the bakery when we're downtown."

Chrissy shook her head. "It's hard for me to understand why people would eat out when they could have eaten at home," she said. "But then back home all the mothers bake every day."

Caroline wasn't sure whether this was meant as a criticism of her mother, so she said nothing but steered Chrissy into the bakery. Caroline noticed that although Chrissy had just eaten an enormous breakfast, she didn't say no to a large croissant with jam and a cup of frothy cappucino, once Caroline explained it was just the Italian word for coffee with steamed milk. After they had sat down at a table, Chrissy didn't take her eyes off the window once. She had a comment for every person who passed them, as if every one of them surprised her. She was especially thrilled when a limo drew up and a chauffeur ran around to open the back door for a lady in mink.

"Is she a movie star or something?" Chrissy asked, wide-eyed.

"I don't think so," Caroline said. "Lots of people in this city have chauffeurs."

"Jeepers!" Chrissy whispered.

When they came out of the bakery, the first person Chrissy spotted was an old man sitting on the sidewalk selling pencils. He had a tin cup beside him, and a scruffy dog was asleep at his feet. Chrissy stared at him, her eyes full of pity.

"Poor man," she whispered. "Can't we give him some money?"

"You shouldn't give beggars money, Chrissy. That's encouraging them. They're all over the city as it is," Caroline said, moving away but feeling a little hard-hearted as she did. "Some of them are really rich. They do this because it's an easy way to make money." Chrissy turned to look back several times as Caroline pulled her past the seated man.

The city's stores were now opening their doors, and Caroline steered Chrissy through the doors of one of the most exclusive ones, even though she had never bought anything there in her life. "Just to show you how the rich people live," Caroline said, trying to pass in through the revolving door as if she always shopped at stores like this.

They wandered to the dress department, and Caroline lifted the tag on a black sequined dress to show to Chrissy. "Eight hundred fifty dollars!" Chrissy squealed. "Mercy! You could buy a heifer for that kind of money." She began going down the racks, lifting up tags, until at last she called out in triumph, "See, here's one I could afford, if I wanted it. It's only sixty-five dollars!"

"That is for the belt, madam," came a discreet voice next to Caroline's ear. "The dress itself is four hundred twenty-five dollars."

Chrissy giggled as they walked away, but Caroline felt herself blushing. She wanted to tell the saleswoman that she was not a dummy who made remarks like that.

"These are the *haute couture* dresses now," she whispered to Chrissy as they walked through glass doors into a small room. "You know, the sort of things wealthy women wear to opening night at the symphony. You don't just pick one out—you have to order it just for yourself."

Chrissy stared at the beaded, sequined, feathered creations with amused interest. "This looks like a suit of armor," she said, giggling. "And this one looks like a person who's been swallowed by an ostrich! Who on earth would wear things like this? People must laugh their heads off!"

Several women in the process of looking at the dresses turned and frowned at Chrissy. Again Caroline wanted to inform them that she wasn't the hick her cousin was. "Let's get out of here, Chrissy," she said. "I think we've seen enough."

"Let's try something that's more my price range now," Chrissy said as she walked out through the revolving door ahead of Caroline. "I mean, there's no use looking if you can't even afford to buy a pair of socks there!"

Her voice trailed off as she finished the sentence, and she grabbed at Caroline's arm. "Caroline, look over there!"

"What? Where?" Caroline asked, sweeping the scene with her eyes for anything unusual.

"That old woman!" Chrissy whispered. "Come on, let's go help her."

"No, Chrissy, wait," Caroline called, but she was too late. Chrissy was already running down the sidewalk toward a filthy old woman who was crouched among enormous shopping bags, attempting to stuff various objects back into one of them.

"Here, let me help you," Caroline heard Chrissy say as she bent down beside the old woman. She began picking up books, bottles, cigarettes, jewelry, pictures, and other items Caroline couldn't quite see and handing them to the old woman.

Caroline hung back in the shadow of the storefront awning, in an agony of indecision. She saw bag ladies like this one every day, shuffling through the streets of the city in their own private world. There were so many homeless people and beggars and drunks that she almost stopped noticing them, except when they shouted and acted crazy and frightened her. Nobody else paid much attention to them either, unless it was a police officer telling them to move on when they sat down.

"Why bless you, dearie," the woman was saying to Chrissy in a husky voice. She looked up at Chrissy and gave her a smile, revealing a mouth full of gaps and blackened teeth. Caroline still stood like a statue, her hands clenched into tight fists. She wanted to go and drag Chrissy away, to tell her that it was never wise or safe to get mixed up with these people, but she also admired the way Chrissy had acted, as if helping strangers were the most natural thing in the world. Deep down, she suspected that Chrissy was behaving the right way and that she, like everyone else in the city, did the wrong thing a hundred times a day.

"You sure do have a lot of stuff here," Chrissy was

saying. "These bags must be heavy. Are you carrying them far?"

The old woman cackled loudly. "I ain't carrying them nowhere, because I've got nowhere to carry them," she said. "I just hang around here most of the time. It's good for a handout."

"You mean you've got nowhere to go?" Chrissy asked.

"That's right," the old woman said. "Everything I've got is in these bags. Sometimes they let me sleep in a shelter at the church. Sometimes not."

"But that's terrible," Chrissy said. "There must be something we can do." She looked up at Caroline. "Can't we take her home for a good meal or something?"

Caroline could feel her cheeks burning with embarrassment. "Chrissy!' she implored, hoping that Chrissy would read in her face that what she was asking was out of the question.

"Well, can't we?" Chrissy demanded again. "I bet you could do with a good meal, couldn't you?"

"Chrissy!" Caroline begged. "Could I talk to you for a minute?"

Chrissy handed the old woman her last item, a battered picture frame with a snapshot of a dog inside it. The woman tucked it into her bag and rose unsteadily to her feet.

"That's all right, dearie. I understand. I'll be on my way again now," she said. She picked up both bags and began to shuffle off, not looking back.

"Caroline, I feel just terrible," Chrissy said angrily,

her eyes still following the shuffling old woman. "How could you just let her go like that?"

Caroline didn't want to admit that she was feeling terrible, too. "Look, Chrissy," she said shakily, "you can't just invite a stranger home for a meal."

"But my mother always feeds tramps," Chrissy said, accusing Caroline with her eyes.

"But it's different in the city." Caroline tried to reason with her. "There are hundreds of homeless people —too many of them for ordinary people like us to help."

"Maybe if we helped just one . . ." Chrissy suggested.

"Chrissy, you don't understand." Caroline tried again. "A lot of them are mentally sick, or on drugs, or alcoholics. There are churches and organizations that take care of them. You have to leave it to them, believe me. You've really got to learn that you have to stay away from strangers in the city, or you could wind up in big trouble."

Chrissy turned to look at her. "If being citified means not caring about other people, then maybe I don't want to learn." She started to walk fast down the block, past the elegant storefronts and the flower vendors' stands. "I don't think I want to see any more right now, Caroline," she said evenly. "Maybe we should go on home for lunch."

"Okay, Chrissy," Caroline said, falling into step beside her. She stared straight ahead of her, feeling both angry and upset. The morning had begun so well. Caroline had felt almost as excited as Chrissy at the prospect of exploring the city. Now that she had seen her own home through someone else's eyes, she was confused and scared.

Darn Chrissy, she thought. *She's only been here less than a day and already she's managed to turn my life upside down.*

Four

The first Saturday evening Chrissy was in San Francisco, she asked, "What time do we go to church tomorrow?"

Caroline, embarrassed to be caught once again in a position Chrissy could criticize, looked across at her mother to answer.

"Oh," Caroline's mother mumbled, "we don't exactly go, Chrissy, but there are enough churches around for us to find you a service any time you want."

"Then I guess I'll go at nine, just like at home," Chrissy said, "if you can give me directions on how to get there."

Caroline was not going to get up on Sunday to walk her cousin to church, and she shot her mother a look that said so.

But her father interrupted the conversation, as if he

sensed what she was thinking. "I'll walk with you, Chrissy," he said, "when I go down to the bakery for our breakfast."

Chrissy rose quietly Sunday morning and dressed in the bathroom, so that Caroline could sleep. But Caroline was a light sleeper and still not used to someone else in her bedroom, so she was awake at eight with Chrissy anyway. She pretended to be asleep, to avoid talking to Chrissy, angry with her cousin and angry at herself for feeling that way.

Are even our Sundays going to be changed from now on? she wondered. *It seems like this one girl has turned our whole life upside down. She'll be back from church and then she'll want to drag us all over the city before we've even read the Sunday comics.*

But when Chrissy returned from her service, just as Caroline's mother was putting on a pot of coffee, she announced, "I'll leave you folks to get on with your breakfast in peace. I've got to write to my boyfriend. It's been five whole days, and I haven't even written one word yet. He'll wonder what terrible things have happened to me."

"Are you sure you don't want to pick up the phone and call?" Caroline's father asked in a kindly way.

Chrissy shook her head. "It's better if I write," she said. "I know what I'm like when I get on the phone with my friends. I'd never want to put it down again, and I don't want to get into the habit of picking up that phone whenever I'm feeling low."

"Okay," Caroline's father said. "Suit yourself. But if you ever feel that you want to call, the phone's right there."

"Thanks, Uncle Richard," Chrissy said, leaping across to give him a hug. "You all are so nice to me."

"Tell you what," he said, squirming free of her hug. "Why don't we all do something this afternoon? It's a nice day. Why don't we get some exercise in Golden Gate Park?"

"What's that?" Chrissy asked.

"It's a huge park," Caroline's father explained. "On Sundays they close it off to traffic, and people go bicycling or roller skating. We could get out your old roller skates, Caroline."

Caroline opened her mouth to say that roller skating was something she had grown out of when she was eleven, but Chrissy shouted, "Oh, wow! Roller skating. That sounds like so much fun! There aren't enough paved roads in Danbury to make roller skating any fun. And the nearest rink is twenty miles off, in Bensonville. I used to do it down the hall at home, but Mom made me stop because I scratched up her polished floors."

"That settles it, then," Caroline's father said, clapping his hands together and looking pleased. "We'll take our bikes down on the bike rack, Edith, and the girls can rent skates at that place next to the park. Then we'll all meet for tea in the tea-garden. Fun afternoon, eh?"

"Oh, yes," Caroline said, rolling her eyes when no one could see her. "Sounds like a blast, Dad."

At least the weather was perfect—unusually clear for San Francisco and not too hot. The park was cool and shady. Its thousands of flowering shrubs were in bloom, and their sweet smell filled the afternoon air. Smiling cyclists and roller skaters cruised down the wide avenues. Traffic was reduced to a distant hum, and birds called to one another among the shrubbery. Only the pleasant swish of wheels on the road surface disturbed the natural rhythms.

After making arrangements to meet the girls later, Caroline's mother and father disappeared on their bicycles, and Caroline and Chrissy sat down together to lace their skates.

"You'll have to help me with this," Chrissy said. "I never became what you'd want to call an expert skater."

"I haven't done it for years, either," Caroline said. "We'll take it easy." She secretly remembered that she had never been the world's best skater either. On junior high trips to the roller rink, Caroline was the one who had inched around the room clinging to the bar on the wall while her friends whizzed by at impossible angles. "Don't worry, Chrissy," she said. "We'll keep to the easy routes, and I'll help you."

They started off slowly down a wide boulevard. A gentle wind blew into their faces as they began to pick up speed.

"Hey, this is fun," Chrissy said. Out of the corner of her eye, Caroline could see that Chrissy was grinning broadly. "If I had a park like this close to my house, I'd be out here every weekend. Do you come here a lot with your friends?"

"Not anymore," Caroline said. She didn't want to admit that her friends thought roller skating was for little kids. "So, did you finish your letter?" she asked.

Again Chrissy beamed. "Yeah, all finished. Five pages of it," she said. "I have to remember to mail it tonight. I hope I get one from Ben pretty soon, even though I know his won't be long like mine. He'll probably only write a few lines about the weather, if I know Ben. He's not exactly the expressive type. But I've never met a man I *could* call the expressive type, have you?"

"I don't know," Caroline said thoughtfully. "Alex and I haven't been going together that long."

"What about your boyfriends before him?"

Caroline hesitated. "I never really had a real boyfriend before him," she said. "I went on dates sometimes, but I never found anyone really special before Alex."

"No kidding?" Chrissy said. "I always thought city girls were real fast. I thought you'd all be dating by eleven."

"Oh, no!" Caroline said. "Most of my friends didn't start dating until end of sophomore year and lots of them still don't have boyfriends. How long have you been going out with Ben?"

"Since eighth grade," Chrissy said. "Most of the girls pair up around then."

"One boy since eighth grade?" Caroline asked. "That sounds so final—like you're going to end up married or something."

"Lots of people do," Chrissy said. "I can name a whole bunch of folks who married their childhood sweethearts."

"And doesn't that worry you?" Caroline asked.

"Now that I think about it, it does," Chrissy said. "I never gave it much thought before. But now I'm real glad I came out here, because it's real easy to slip into the routine of having a guy around. Mind you, Ben's the best sort of guy to have around. He's fun, and he's thoughtful. He said he didn't want to hold me back from coming out here, even though I could tell he hated it."

"What about dating other people while you're away?" Caroline asked.

"I don't imagine he'll want to do that," Chrissy said. "People would talk."

Caroline shook her head. "I can't see any boy I know staying faithful to a girl who's gone for a year," she said. "Most of the kids around here don't even stick to one person for more than a few months."

"How long have you stuck to Alex?" Chrissy asked, with a grin.

Caroline felt herself blushing, as she often did when she thought about Alex. "Oh, we only started going together in May," she said hesitantly. "And he's been away for a lot of the summer, so there hasn't been much sticking to do."

"I'm dying to meet him," Chrissy said. "All I've got from you so far is tall, dark, handsome, and mysterious. That's enough to drive me wild with curiosity!"

"Where did you get the idea he was mysterious?" Caroline asked.

Chrissy grinned. "Well, every time I ask you about him, you shut up like a clam, so I figured there had to be something mysterious about him. Maybe he's thirty-five or he's a famous rock star."

Caroline laughed. "Chrissy, you have the wildest imagination," she said. "He's very normal really, I suppose, but I wouldn't call him ordinary. It's just that it's hard for me to describe him without sounding corny. You'll meet him soon, anyway."

"I hope so," Chrissy said. "I might have to practice my flirting on him, just so I don't forget by next summer!"

"You'd better not," Caroline said, again made uneasy by Chrissy's innocent joke. Hadn't Alex said the same thing—that he was waiting to flirt with Chrissy? *I wish they wouldn't tease like that*, she thought. *I know they're both only kidding but it's hard to laugh it off when it's my first real boyfriend and my cousin is such a great-looking girl!*

"You don't have to worry yourself," Chrissy said. "After all, I'd hardly stand a chance against someone as beautiful as you."

Caroline glanced at her cousin in amazement, wondering if Chrissy was still teasing. Never once in her life had she thought of herself as beautiful. But Chrissy's eyes no longer had that teasing twinkle in them. Caroline steadied herself on her skates, shaking back her hair and pretending that she was used to compliments like that.

"Well, you and Alex will get a chance to meet next week," she said. "He's due back then."

"From where?" Chrissy asked.

Caroline grinned. "Right now he's walking over mountains with fifty pounds on his back."

"Holy mazoley," Chrissy said.

Caroline laughed. "You know, you say the funniest things," she said.

"So do you!"

"I do not!"

"What about all those foreign things like *Ciao* or *Mon Dieu* or whatever?"

"I guess I do!" Caroline admitted. "I'd never thought of it before. Maybe it's something we both inherited!"

Chrissy laughed. "Hey, that's terrific! That really makes me feel like we belong together. *Woooo!*" she screamed as her legs shot out from under her. Caroline grabbed her, teetered, and went down beside her. They both sat on the pavement for a second, Caroline crimson with embarrassment that anyone might see her in this undignified position. Then Chrissy burst out laughing.

"When I said we belonged together, I didn't mean for you to follow me into all my disasters!"

In spite of herself, Caroline found that she was laughing, too. "I didn't mean to," she said. "I guess I'm a bit rusty on skates. My legs just wouldn't go the way I wanted them to!"

"Are you okay?"

"Sure. I'm fine. How about you?"

"My backside is a little sore. Otherwise I'm terrific," Chrissy said. "Come on, let's get going again!" She tried to get to her feet. "This isn't as easy as it looks," she complained. "Give me a hand, will you?"

Caroline tried to stand, but her skates wouldn't co-operate. She had to turn onto her knees, brace herself with her hands, and then push herself up very slowly before she was finally standing—just in time to see two gorgeous blond guys on bikes laughing at her as they rolled by. Caroline felt her face go hot as her legs wob-bled from embarrassment and fear of falling again.

Chrissy watched her from the ground, shaking with laughter.

"You're as bad as I am, Caroline Kirby! We must look awful funny, crawling around on the pavement!"

Caroline was about to defend herself and put the blame on rusty skates or slippery asphalt, but instead she found herself giggling along with Chrissy as they both finally stood up and started skating again. Chrissy didn't care at all about how people looked. She didn't mind if someone saw her making a fool of herself. Caroline found herself looking at Chrissy with envy. How nice it would be to feel so sure of yourself that you didn't care what other people thought! *Will I ever have that sort of confidence?* Caroline wondered. *And is it really confidence, or is she just too naive to realize that other people think she's weird?*

They turned a corner and found themselves at the top of a long hill.

"Hey, Cara, you know what?" Chrissy asked, coming to a halt and clutching her cousin's arm.

"No, what?"

"I don't know how to go down hills."

"You know what, Chrissy?"

"No, what?"

"Neither do I!"

"I've got a good idea," Chrissy suggested. "Why don't we walk down the edge of the flower beds?"

"Good idea," Caroline agreed. They carefully began to make their way along the soft earth. They were about halfway down when a loud voice stopped them.

"Hey, you there, get off my flowers!" An elderly park attendant ran toward them, waving a rake.

"Quick, run!" Chrissy said, grabbing Caroline's arm and starting to totter off across the grass. Caroline followed, stumbling as the wheel of her skates sank into the earth. Once they were hidden behind a screen of bushes, she looked back, then grabbed at Chrissy.

"What are we running for?" she asked. "He's not following us."

"Oh, isn't he?" Chrissy started to giggle again.

"You know, we are fools," Caroline said, shaking her head in disbelief. "I have both our shoes here in my backpack. We don't have to stagger any farther."

"Good idea," Chrissy said, sinking to the grass to take off her skates. Once she had removed them, Chrissy lay back on the grass. "Let's just fan the roller skating for today, okay?" she asked.

"Fine with me," Caroline agreed. "We've got to move a little faster than we were on skates, anyway, or we'll never be on time to meet my parents. The tea garden is on the other side of the park."

As the girls walked across the park, they passed a small pond where little boys and serious old men were sailing model boats that ranged from carved blocks of wood to scale models of ocean liners. Above the buzz of conversation came the sobs of one little boy who leaned over the wall that bordered the pond.

Chrissy immediately ran to his side. "What's the matter, honey?" she asked. The little boy said nothing but pointed to a tiny sailboat, capsized and being carried by the breeze to the middle of the pond.

"Here, hold on. I'll get it for you," Chrissy volunteered, slipping off her shoes.

"Chrissy, what are you doing?" Caroline asked.

"I'm going to get his boat," Chrissy said. "Hold these, please."

"But you can't just . . ." Caroline began. But Chrissy could. She stepped into the knee-deep water and began to wade toward the boat. Caroline watched helplessly from the shore. Everyone else on shore was watching too, cheering Chrissy or making fun of her. One spectator was getting more and more agitated.

"Hey, watch out!" a man in a yachting cap called. Chrissy turned too late to see a model ocean liner bearing down on her.

"Whoa," she yelled, trying to step out of the way. The wave she created met the liner head on. The ship bucked and then was engulfed. The man on the bank was spluttering and croaking. His face was purple.

"I'm sorry," Chrissy called. "But I think I just sank the *Titanic!*"

The other spectators cheered as Chrissy rescued both boats and carried them back to shore. Caroline couldn't help grinning. Chrissy staggered back to shore, one boat held high in the air in each hand. She winced as her feet touched the muddy bottom of the pond. As she climbed up on land, Caroline caught sight of the sign: NO WADING. Fine $25.

"Let's get out of here," Caroline said, helping Chrissy over the wall. "We're late for my parents at the tea garden."

"Just a minute," Chrissy said. She knelt by the little boy. "Here," she said, holding out his boat to him. "As good as new." She was about to hand it to him but drew it back. "Oh-oh!" she said. She rubbed the boat on her jeans to remove a speck of mud from the side.

"Come on, please, Chrissy," Caroline pleaded. She was conscious of the eyes of a hundred spectators watching Chrissy and her.

"Okay. We had to make sure the boat was clean, didn't we?" Chrissy asked the little boy. He nodded and stared after Chrissy wide-eyed as she grinned at him and ran to join Caroline. Caroline glanced back over her shoulder, half expecting a park policeman to be running after them with a ticket. Things like park regulations didn't seem to bother Chrissy. *Only people*, Caroline thought. *She really cares about people.*

Caroline's parents were waiting in a small pagoda at the top of the tea garden. The girls climbed together over humpbacked bridges and past waterfalls and stone lanterns, until they both sat down breathlessly on one of the pagoda's low seats.

"I could certainly use some tea," Caroline said, taking the cup of steaming green liquid from her mother.

"What sort of tea is this?" Chrissy asked, peering down at hers suspiciously.

"Green tea," Mr. Kirby explained. "Haven't you tasted it in Chinese restaurants?"

Chrissy made a face. "The nearest Chinese restaurant is a good fifty miles away from us. But even if we were close to it, I don't think we'd ever go. My dad and brothers are real meat-and-potato men. When my mom tries out a recipe from a woman's magazine, they get real suspicious."

"Then we'd better wind up tonight at a Chinese restaurant," Mrs. Kirby suggested. "Good idea, Richard?"

"Great idea," he said. "Now, did you two girls have a fun afternoon?"

"It was great, Uncle Richard," Chrissy said immediately.

Caroline played the day rapidly through in her mind. She recalled falling down on roller skates and giggling uncontrollably as she tried to stand. She thought about being chased by the park caretaker. She pictured the purple face of the man whose boat Chrissy had sunk and the pleasure in the eyes of the little boy whose boat she had rescued. None of the things that had happened that afternoon would have been what her friends called fun. In fact, she was pretty sure her friends would have been among the people who stood by the pond laughing at Chrissy. Yet Caroline knew she had had fun. She had giggled. She had stretched contentedly in the grass. She had definitely had a good time.

"Yes, Dad," she said. "We did have a fun afternoon."

[illegible]

[illegible] possessed. [illegible]

[illegible] It was just as well [illegible]

[illegible]

[illegible]

[illegible]

Five

"Chrissy?" Caroline called. She stood in the empty hallway of the apartment and listened for a sound. There was no answer. Caroline sighed. Her first week in San Francisco, Chrissy had befriended a bag lady, nearly fallen off a cable car, and waded illegally in Golden Gate Park. By her second week, she'd gotten lost in Chinatown and practically started a fistfight. Now she was nowhere in sight and two hours late. Wouldn't the chaos she created ever end?

"Chrissy? Are you home yet?" she called again.

The door to her father's study opened, and his head, glasses on the end of his nose as usual, poked around the door. "What's the matter?" he asked. "Something wrong, or do you usually call the fire department without using the telephone?"

"Sorry if I disturbed you, Dad," Caroline said with

a grin at her father's befuddled face. "It's Chrissy again. I left her two hours ago outside Macy's. I told her what bus to catch and then I went to my ballet class. She said she'd go straight home."

"Don't worry," Mr. Kirby said. "I expect she got held up window-shopping again. You know that girl goes bonkers when she sees all those clothes in the store windows."

"I just hope something hasn't happened to her again," Caroline said, dropping her dance bag with a thump onto the polished floor. "Really Dad, I'll have gray hair by the time she leaves."

Her father laughed. "Give her time to settle in, then she'll be fine. I bet it would take you awhile to know what you were doing on a farm. Chrissy's got to learn the city ropes."

"Yes, but why does she always have to learn the hard way?" Caroline asked. "I ask you, Dad, what am I going to do with her? She talks to strange people on buses, she tried to break up a fight between two punks, she helped a drunk who had fallen over in the gutter. The way she's going, she won't survive the year."

Mr. Kirby laughed again. "She has a good heart, that's all. She's just a very friendly girl, and she hasn't learned yet that you can't be too friendly with some city people."

"I wonder what she's done this time." Caroline sighed. "Do you think she's rounding up some junkies to bring home for dinner? Maybe she's lecturing some cop for being mean to a bum?" Caroline frowned, thinking of the trouble Chrissy might really be getting into. "Do you think I should go look for her? Oh, I'm so tired.

Getting back into serious dance practice is no joke. My legs would hardly make it up the stairs."

"You go take your shower, honey," her father said, turning back to his room again. "She'll be back. That girl has great survival instincts. Whatever happens to her, I have a feeling she'll come through just fine."

"I hope you're right," Caroline said. "I feel so responsible for her." She picked up her dance bag and walked to her bedroom. On Chrissy's bed was a pile of jeans and shirts, her towel, and her hairbrush. Caroline mechanically picked up the clothes and sorted them between clothes hamper and closet. Then she straightened up a half-written letter on Chrissy's desk top that was about to fall to the floor. For a moment, she was tempted to read it, but she fought the temptation and covered the top sheet with a box of envelopes. She was only too aware how hard it was to have a stranger invading her own privacy—taking up her living space and intruding on her thoughts.

Although I'd love to know what you think about me, Chrissy . . . I wonder if you think I'm as hard to understand as I think you are. Do you know that you don't make any sense to me? You're always leaping up to help around the house and making me feel guilty in the process, but you're the biggest slob when it comes to your own room. You obviously care a lot about people, because I've seen you do so many kind, crazy things. But you obviously have no idea how many things you do that embarrass me.

She hung her ballet bag on its hook, then fished out her leotard and threw it into the dirty-clothes hamper. Then she headed to the bathroom for a long, soothing shower. But even under the hot, pulsing spray, she could only worry about Chrissy.

"I'll be gray before I turn seventeen," Caroline muttered, examining herself in her mirror as she toweled her hair. But why did she even care where Chrissy was? Nobody had told her, after all, that she was responsible for Chrissy's well-being. *The trouble is,* Caroline thought, *it's hard not to like you and to care about you. Oh, I hope you're okay right now.*

"Caroline, Richard, somebody?" Her mother's voice rang down the hall. "Come and give me a hand here before I collapse!"

Caroline slipped on her robe and hurried toward her mother's urgent calls.

"Here, take these cold cuts," her mother directed. "Look at the time. Nothing's done yet! I bet you didn't even think to straighten up the living room." She looked at Caroline's blank face. "Don't tell me you both forgot about the cocktail party?"

"Oh," Caroline said. "The party. This is the night you have the showing for that new artist Fernando What's-His-Name."

"Right," her mother said with a tight-lipped smile. "And do you also remember that I happened to mention before I left this morning that I would appreciate a little help in getting ready for twenty guests?"

"I'm sorry, Mom," Caroline mumbled. "I remembered on the way home from ballet, but then I got home, and Chrissy wasn't here, and I started to worry about her."

Mrs. Kirby looked up sharply. "Chrissy wasn't here? Is she back now?"

"Not yet," Caroline said. "I left her at the right bus stop, Mom. That was two hours ago."

"Oh, no." Her mother sighed. "I need this like a hole in the head. We'd better call the police, Richard."

"Give her awhile," Mr. Kirby said calmly. "There might be a perfectly reasonable explanation. She might have seen something in a store window and wandered inside. After all, it's only five-thirty. Young ladies of sixteen are allowed to be out alone at five-thirty, you know."

"But not straight from the farm, Richard. You know she's capable of getting lost. What are we going to do?"

"We'll get your party all prepared. Then, if she's still not home, Caroline and I will take the car and go looking for her," Mr. Kirby said, still calmly. "But frankly, I can't think that too much could happen to somebody in the middle of downtown, in the middle of the afternoon. Caroline, help your mother with the food, and I'll gather up the newspapers."

Caroline wandered after her mother into the kitchen and mechanically began arranging cold cuts on platters. She wasn't so sure as her father that nothing bad could have happened to Chrissy yet. "Drat her and double drat her," she muttered, throwing olives at the platter of meats she had just finished arranging. "She's done nothing but turn this place upside down since she landed. The trouble is that I do feel responsible for her. I'd be the one they'd blame if anything did happen to her!" As if Caroline could ever control Chrissy, anyway.

She thought of the incident with Chrissy she had decided not to tell her parents about. Chrissy certainly had shown she could take care of herself then. The girls had gone to a late show at the theater three blocks from their apartment. When they came out of the movie it was late, and the streets were practically deserted. Caroline had noticed the two guys in the shadows as they came out of the theater. They were the same two guys she had noticed earlier eyeing her as she got in line for popcorn. They were both dressed in a lot of studded leather, and they both wore spiky, punk haircuts.

"Hey, gorgeous," one of them called out as they fell into step behind the girls. "What's the big hurry?"

"Ignore them," Caroline whispered. "They'll lose interest if we pretend they aren't there."

But the two guys did not lose interest. They only got more persistent as the street became more deserted. *Chrissy must be terrified by this*, Caroline thought. *I bet she's never had this sort of thing happen in Iowa.*

"Let's just walk faster," she whispered to Chrissy. "We can sprint the last block."

But they had to pause at a cross street as a car turned, and one of the guys grabbed at Caroline's arm. "Hey baby," he growled. "Where you going? What's the big hurry?"

"Will you get your hands off me," Caroline said, trying to sound calm even though she knew her voice was quavering. "I am not the least bit interested in you or your friend. I'm not your type, and you are wasting your time."

"I'll tell you what my type is—female!" the guy said, laughing at his own joke. "And I don't take no for an answer. My bike's parked just down here. Let's go for a little ride."

"I think you should know that I live on this block," Caroline said. "If I shout for help, the police will be here in seconds."

The guy laughed again. "Oh, wow," he said. "I'm real scared."

Then the other guy grabbed at Chrissy. "Hey, beautiful. I bet you ain't so hard to get," he said. Chrissy knocked his hand from her arm instantly and glared at him.

"Listen, creeps," she said. "You must be real thick if you don't get the message yet. We don't like you. We don't want to know you better. We think you look disgusting, and we wouldn't talk to you if you were the last two guys on earth. Now do you understand?"

The guy moved toward her again. "I like a good wrestle with a foxy girl," he began. But he never finished the sentence, because Chrissy had grabbed his right arm and twisted herself out of his grasp before he knew what was happening to him.

"Don't push me too far," she threatened. "I've wrestled a good many hogs to the ground and one hog weighs more than both of you put together. Where I come from girls know how to keep animals away. Now get lost. Fast."

She gave the boy a hefty shove, so that he staggered a few paces down the street. He turned back to look at her in astonishment. "Come on," he said. "They ain't worth hanging around for. Let's go find ourselves some real women!"

Then the punks turned and swaggered off, leaving

Caroline shaking with fright and Chrissy with a big grin on her face. "I said I could deck them, and I really could have," she told Caroline.

"You were terrific," Caroline had to admit. "You got both of us out of an ugly situation."

"You do learn a few things on the farm," Chrissy said, smiling to herself as if she knew that Caroline usually thought she was a hick.

They had walked the rest of the way home in silence. Caroline was deep in her own thoughts. She had always believed that adults handled difficult moments with reason, calmness, and dignity. Yet here was Chrissy, threatening violence and hurling insults and winning where Caroline had failed.

Nothing has made sense since Chrissy got here, Caroline decided, as she dressed mechanically for the party in the quiet of her room. *For the past sixteen years I've been trying to turn myself into one of those cool, sophisticated girls who float down the halls at school. Now, just when it seems I might be getting a little closer to maturity and sophistication, Chrissy arrives and acts just about as unsophisticated as you can get. Yet she breaks every rule I've thought was important and she's happier than anyone else I know.*

A car drew up outside, and Caroline heard a door slam. She hurried to the window and peered out. Two elegantly dressed people were coming up the steps. She sighed and turned away. *I just hope she has gotten away with it this time*, Caroline thought, biting at her bottom lip.

In a few minutes, people started arriving regularly for the party. The sculptor Fernando arrived and set up his work on the dining table. Caroline found a spot by the window and guarded it carefully. "Do you think we should go look for her yet, Dad?" she whispered when the streetlights outside came on.

"Maybe we should," her father agreed. "I'll tell your mother we're going."

As he turned away, Caroline glanced out the window again. A large, yellow fire truck was pulling up outside the house. As she watched, the truck door opened. Caroline knew what was coming next. In a few moments, Chrissy jumped down, waved to the men on the truck, and began to run up the steps.

"Okay, surprise me," Caroline said dryly, meeting her in the front hall. "You helped put out a fire and saved the city from burning. In gratitude, the San Francisco Fire Department has given you a truck as your personal taxi."

Chrissy giggled. "You are funny," she said. "It's a lot simpler than that. I got on the wrong bus—"

"You hailed a fire truck by mistake? Next time look for the number on the front. Buses have numbers, fire trucks do not," Caroline said.

"Oh, I got on the right number bus all right," Chrissy said, missing or ignoring Caroline's sarcasm. "Only I didn't know that you didn't mean the express bus. You told me to get off after four stops, but this bus didn't stop even once until it got way out into the boonies right down by the docks. I had spent all my money except my bus fare on this cute little tank top, so I couldn't call you or get back again. Then I saw a fire station, so I went in and asked to use their phone. They were so sweet, Caroline. They gave me a soda, then they said they had to go out to test the engine anyway, so they'd drive me home."

"Terrific," Caroline said. "Do you realize you had us all worried sick?"

Chrissy looked astonished. "Gee, I'm sorry," she said. "But you really don't have to worry about me, Caroline. I can take care of myself just fine." She walked into the living room but stopped short when she saw the roomful of people. "What's this all about?" she whispered.

"It's one of Mom's private showings," Caroline whispered back. "There's some good food."

But Chrissy was staring in horror at the dining table. "Hey, Caroline," she said. "What is that pile of junk doing there? Your mother will die of embarrassment if she sees it. Should I take it away before I change my clothes?"

"Junk?" Caroline asked. "What junk?"

People standing close to them looked up with interest. Chrissy continued to stare at the table. "That stuff on the dining-room table," she said, pointing at it. "It looks ike your Dad was taking an engine apart or something. Let's get it out of here."

"Chrissy! That's the work of art they've all come to see," Caroline said in a shocked voice. "That's the sort of work Fernando is famous for."

"That's art?" Chrissy asked, her eyes opening very wide. "That old motor bike engine?"

Caroline was aware of all the eyes upon them. She nodded and said patiently, "It's a piece of sculpture called 'Death and Rebirth.'"

"Holy cow!" Chrissy said. Caroline looked from her face to the sculpture and started to laugh.

"What's so funny?" the woman beside her asked. "May we share the joke?"

"She thought the sculpture was an engine my dad was working on," Caroline confided. Pretty soon the joke had spread all around the room.

"I think I'll go change," Chrissy said with dignity. "You get really dirty on buses." She turned to go, her head high, shoulders thrown back, and cheeks very pink. The sight of Chrissy so wounded turned Caroline's amusement to guilt. *What made me do that?* she asked herself. *Was I just trying to get even because she had worried me so much? Or because I'm jealous that everything always seems to turn out so well for her?*

Caroline didn't like either possibility. She quickly grabbed a plate of food and headed after Chrissy. "Here," she said. "I'll bet you're hungry after your grand tour of the dockland. If you wait until you've had a shower, those guys in there will have cleaned up. Artists who create with motor bike engines always have large appetites."

Chrissy took the plate without saying anything, but after a moment she offered Caroline a broad smile.

Six

Caroline made her way slowly up the steepest part of the hill to her house. Her first Saturday rehearsal session for the ballet's performing company had left her with barely enough strength to put one foot in front of the other. Every muscle in her body had gone on strike. Even her head felt fragile after three hours of Madame's thumping on the floor with her fat stick and shouting commands rapid-fire. Every word echoed in Caroline's skull.

The biggest trouble was that none of the other students seemed to suffer the way Caroline did. The girls on both sides at rehearsal had calmly followed Madame's barrage of instructions. They never moved in the wrong direction or bumped into people as Caroline once had done. And they didn't seem to mind Madame's constant criticism, either.

If I'm ever going to be a real ballerina, I've got to get used to it, Caroline admitted to herself. *I've got to stop being sensitive. One of these days I'm going to burst into tears in front of everyone and make a fool of myself.*

The girl beside Caroline had gone right on dancing while Madame shouted that she had seen sacks of potatoes landing more gracefully. When Madame had singled Caroline out to ask if she could remember which foot was her left, Caroline had hardly dared to look up, afraid to meet the stares of the rest of the class.

But she had survived it without collapsing or bursting into tears, and now Caroline was looking forward to a long, lazy afternoon in the sun. It was the first really hot day in weeks. The cloudless sky was deep blue, and the bay was dotted with white sails.

I hope Chrissy won't want to do anything too energetic, Caroline thought.

Life with Chrissy had been relatively quiet in the past few days. At least she hadn't arrived home in any more fire trucks. It even had been pleasant lately to have someone around in the evenings. Caroline's parents often went out to concerts or art shows and left the girls alone in the apartment. Even watching TV was less of a bore if someone else watched with you. And Chrissy would often volunteer to get up and make popcorn or a huge triple-decker sandwich for them both, something that never seemed worth the trouble for one person when Caroline was all alone.

I guess I'm getting used to having her around, Caroline decided. She no longer minded so much when she found Chrissy's clothing on the floor or started when

Chrissy yelled down the hall that breakfast was ready. *This year may work out just fine*, she thought.

What Caroline saw in front of her house wiped all thoughts of Chrissy out of her mind. She wasn't sure she recognized the license plate, but surely no two people who would park on this block could have a bright blue VW Bug with a Rolls-Royce front. Alex was home early. And he had come to see her.

Caroline's heart bounded. Alex was back! Alex was upstairs waiting for her. She took the flight of steps from the street two at a time. At the top of the steps was a big porch, hidden from the street, where the girls did their sunbathing. As Caroline approached it, she saw that somebody was sitting on the floor of the porch. Then she saw that it was two somebodies. She instantly recognized the soft hair curled at the back of the neck in front of her. Alex was squatting on a beach blanket hovering closely over Chrissy, who wore the tiniest Hawaiian-print bikini Caroline ever had seen. Caroline couldn't read Alex's expression, but Chrissy's would have been impossible to miss. She was gazing up at Alex with a look of total adoration.

Caroline had turned to stone. She willed herself to move or to speak, but her legs wouldn't carry her, and her mouth wouldn't make any sound. Her heart was hammering so loudly that she was sure both of them would hear it and turn around. But it was only too clear they hadn't even noticed her coming. Caroline watched silently as Alex patted Chrissy's hand and said brightly, "So don't forget, it's a date, okay?"

"Okay," Chrissy began. Then she looked up and

saw Caroline. Alex turned with her to stare at her. Guilt was pasted all over both of their faces.

"Welcome home, Alex," Caroline said in a strained voice. "What a nice surprise. I thought you weren't coming back until Tuesday."

Alex moved away from Chrissy and scrambled to his feet. "Hi, Cara," he said. "I got back early. We got caught in a three-day thunderstorm, and we ran out of dry clothes and food, so my dad finally admitted we could quit. I can't tell you how good the first signs of civilization looked. We staggered into a gas station, and I got a soda from the machine. Boy, was that great. We got back this morning. I just stopped at home for a shower and then I came by to surprise you. But you weren't here."

"Well, I see you met Chrissy instead," Caroline said, fighting to keep her voice calm and even. "I was thinking that I'd have to get you guys together to introduce you. But now I don't have to. That's just great."

"Alex thought I was you," Chrissy said, grinning up at Caroline. How easily she recovered after being caught red-handed. "He crept up to surprise you, only he got the surprise, because it was me."

"I had no idea we looked so much alike," Caroline said.

"From behind," Alex said rapidly. "Chrissy's hair looks kind of like yours when it's down over her shoulders. And I wasn't expecting to meet anybody else who looked like you lying in a bikini on your porch."

"He scared me half out of my wits, I can tell you," Chrissy said hastily. "I was lying down reading and suddenly this strange man grabs me and whispers, 'I've got you, you gorgeous creature. You are my prisoner.' I remembered everything you ever told me about all the weirdos who live in big cities. But when I screamed that I'd call the cops, he was more surprised than I had been."

"Surprised?" Alex said with a good-natured grin at Chrissy. "I was terrified. Luckily Chrissy isn't the sort of girl who panics. Otherwise, I might have been in jail by now."

"Anyway, when we both finally figured who we were talking to, we got along just great," Chrissy said.

"I could see that," Caroline said. Chrissy didn't seem to notice the icy tone in Caroline's voice, but Alex began squirming again.

"She was . . . er . . . just telling me about her family at home and how much she misses them and—"

"It's okay, Alex," Caroline cut in. "You don't have to explain yourself to me. So you met Chrissy. I'm glad. Why don't we all go up and get something to drink? My mouth feels like sandpaper after two hours of ballet and the walk up the hill."

"You two go up," Chrissy said awkwardly. "I expect you don't need me to bug you after you've been apart practically all summer. Besides, I want to work on my tan some more, and I've been meeting some interesting people down here today."

Caroline saw that Alex flashed Chrissy a quick smile before he followed Caroline into the house.

Inside the apartment, Alex took Caroline's arm. "Hey, what's bugging you?" he asked. "Is this any way to greet a guy who's been brushing with death on top of mountains?"

Caroline turned to him, studying his face carefully. "I'm sorry, Alex," she said. "I was just—I was a little surprised seeing you and Chrissy together like that."

A big grin crossed Alex's face. "That's what I like," he teased. "Two women fighting over me. Keep 'em jealous, I always say."

"Don't tease about things like that, Alex," Caroline said. "It's not funny."

Alex pulled her close to him. "Well, you must at least be happy one of your worries did not come true," he said. "Chrissy is not what I'd call a hillbilly. That bikini didn't look like a farm-girl costume to me. In fact I'd swear I saw a designer label on it."

"You certainly were observing it very closely," Caroline said frostily. "In fact, if you two had been sitting any closer together, you'd have bumped noses."

Alex slid his arms around her waist and pulled her in tight. "You crazy coot," he whispered. "Did you really think I was making a play for Chrissy? I was just talking to her, waiting for you to get home."

"Ha!" Caroline said, leaning away from him. "Is that what it was? Talking?"

Alex looked down at her tenderly. "Believe it or not, that's what it was. Cara, what did you think I thought about, stranded up there in the mountains during a thunderstorm? I thought, if only Caroline were up here with me, it wouldn't be half so bad. We'd cuddle together in a tiny tent. The rain drumming on the roof would even seem romantic." He paused and looked at her with big, serious eyes. "I missed you, Cara," he said. "I counted the days until I could see you again."

"I missed you, too, Alex," Caroline whispered.

"So how about a welcome-home kiss?" he asked. "I've been here ten minutes with my lips all puckered up." He made a funny face, and Caroline had to laugh.

"You dope," she said. "Here, is this better?" She tilted her face toward his and they moved together.

"Much better," he whispered as they drew apart. "That was fine for openers. Now for the main course."

"Alex," Caroline warned. "We're not in the house alone, you know. My father or my cousin might come in at any moment."

"So they can watch a good demonstration of kissing," Alex said, smiling down at her. "I bet your cousin Chrissy wouldn't push me away in such a hurry. I hear they're very warm and eager down on the farm."

Caroline stiffened in his arms. "Hey, I was only teasing," he said. "Boy, you *are* uptight today. How about if we go out together somewhere tonight. Just the two of us. Would that make you feel better?"

"I can't tonight, Alex," Caroline began.

"I know. Ballet practice." Alex said forlornly.

Caroline had to smile at his look. "Not tonight. My father's taking us all to the opera. It's Chrissy's first opera. I get a feeling I'll have to tell her what's going on in every scene."

Alex grinned. "You don't need to know what's going on in operas. The girl falls in love with the wrong boy, somebody stabs her, and the boy kills himself. Simple."

"Oh, Alex." Caroline laughed. "I wish I could come out with you this evening, but I really can't."

"Tomorrow, then?" he asked. "We'll go for a drive someplace."

"Okay," Caroline said. "That would be great."

"I'll call you in the morning," Alex said. "Maybe we'll take a picnic."

After he had gone, Caroline watched through the kitchen window as Alex disappeared down the hill, running with easy strides down the steep slope toward his car. "Oh, Alex," she said. "Why did I let you go like that? I made it clear I didn't want you to hang around this afternoon, when all I've dreamed of since you left is having you back again."

Chrissy crossing the porch in her bikini caught Caroline's eye. She tensed. *That's what's wrong*, she thought. *Is she going to spoil things with Alex, too? He swears he wasn't making a play for her, but was she making a play for him?* Caroline recalled what she had seen when she came up the steps. No matter what Alex said, he and Chrissy had been talking about a date. Caroline had heard every word. "Chrissy Madden," Caroline said to the figure approaching the door, "I wish I'd never heard I had a long-lost cousin."

Seven

"So this is an opera house!" Chrissy exclaimed. "I can hardly believe it. It's so elegant, it's like being in a movie. Look at those chandeliers! And the carpet on the stairs! We should be drifting down the staircase in long, flowing dresses ready to meet a prince or something!"

"Some people do wear long, flowing dresses," Caroline said. "If you look down at the really expensive seats or over at the boxes, you'll see quite a few gowns and lots of minks."

"I wish I had something more fancy than this," Chrissy said, looking down at her lace-edged, cotton sundress. "I hope everyone doesn't stare at me and wonder what I'm doing here."

"Of course they won't," Caroline said, slightly impatiently. "In this city you can wear what you like. You can come to the opera in jeans if you want to. People have bigger things on their minds than what you're wearing."

"But you all look just right," Chrissy said, eyeing Caroline's sleek black-and-electric-blue satin dress with the huge padded shoulders and her mother's embroidered silk gown hanging in elegant folds. "I really do feel like the country cousin."

"You look fine, Chrissy," Caroline said. "Come on, let's get to our seats. I want to have time to read the program." Chrissy obediently followed her uncle and aunt up the stairs.

Caroline hurried to catch up with her family. They had seats in the middle of the grand tier—the first balcony—with a perfect view of the stage, the orchestra, and the opera-goers below them. Chrissy swiveled in her seat like a little kid, gazing at the ornate ceiling, the draped boxes, the extravagant chandeliers, and the elegantly dressed people—commenting on each in turn. Caroline tried to share Chrissy's delight in everything, but tonight of all nights Chrissy's act of country innocence really annoyed her.

How could anybody be so enthusiastic about everything? she wondered. *Was Chrissy for real, or was the helpless little girl fresh from the farm an act she put on to get attention?* Of course Chrissy wasn't trying to get attention. She was just bubbly and outgoing and delighted by every new thing she saw. *And totally the opposite of me*, Caroline thought with a sigh.

Caroline had come to this realization earlier in the afternoon, as she lay on her bed trying to rest for the evening. Then she had used it to comfort herself: No boy who was interested in her could also be interested in Chrissy, since they had nothing but a few—very few—genes in common. But somehow as she watched her cousin this evening, the thought was not very comforting.

"If you want to know the story, you'd better read your program," she leaned over to tell Chrissy. "Otherwise you won't know what's going on."

"Why not?" Chrissy asked.

"Because they're going to sing in German," Caroline said.

Chrissy's eyes opened wide. "What for?"

"Because the opera is written in German. They nearly always sing it in the original language here."

"But then nobody can understand it," Chrissy commented.

"Everybody reads the program first," Caroline said, opening hers. Chrissy opened hers, too, but almost immediately the lights were lowered and the conductor made his appearance. Chrissy sat entranced through the overture. Then the curtain went up to reveal a woodland scene with a primitive hut. As the action unfolded, Caroline occasionally peeked over at Chrissy to see how she was reacting to the show. Her smile first faded into a look of determined concentration, then to a frown, then to a look of hopeless confusion. Finally Caroline heard a loud shifting accompanied by a long sigh in the seat next to her.

"What's happening?" Chrissy asked her in a loud whisper.

"The man is lost, and he's asking the woman for a

drink of water," Caroline said. Chrissy nodded and went back to listening. Another ten minutes passed.

"What's happening now?" Chrissy asked.

"She's saying that she'll get him one," Caroline whispered. Chrissy looked horrified. "It will be midnight before he's even had a drink at this rate," she said. Her voice was high and clear, and although she thought she was whispering, several people in front of her turned around. Some said, "Shhh!" Others stifled smiles. Caroline's face flushed.

The opera progressed. Caroline explained that the man was the woman's long-lost brother, but she didn't know it. They were falling in love, and that made the gods angry.

"But that doesn't seem fair," Chrissy said. "If you ask me, this story would be much better without the gods. They keep on interfering."

Again the people in front of them turned around, and some of them grinned. Caroline shot Chrissy a quick look, then lowered her head behind her program, in embarrassment. She didn't want the other theatergoers to think she was a total beginner at opera as well.

"Wagner is always full of gods interfering," she whispered.

"I think I liked *Oklahoma!* better," Chrissy muttered. "At least that had pieces you could sing along with."

Again Caroline cringed. She longed for the opera to be over and to get safely home. She looked down at her watch several times during the last act, hoping that they could make it to the end without any more commentary from Chrissy.

The opera finally climbed toward its climax. The chief of the gods had persuaded the evil king to kill the woman who had left him to find the man she loved—her secret brother. The king grabbed the woman in the forest and thrust a knife into her as she sang. She slowly sank to the ground, lifeless and silent. The king and the hero looked together silently at her lifeless body. Chrissy turned to Caroline again and broke the complete quiet in the theater. "I don't really blame him, do you? I'd stab her, too, if she were singing in my ear all night like that."

Chrissy had intended to whisper to Caroline, but her clear voice carried through the theater. A ripple of laughter went through the grand tier seats around them. Caroline's face burned with embarrassment. As the curtain came down, she pushed out of her seat and past her family and fled to the parking lot.

The girls rode home in uncomfortable silence. Caroline sat as far as possible from Chrissy in the backseat, staring out of the window as if she were fascinated by the scenery. Caroline's father made attempts at jolly conversation. Caroline could feel Chrissy turn toward her a couple of times, but her head remained turned firmly away.

It's no use, she thought. *She hasn't changed at all. I thought she was beginning to fit in here. I thought she'd be just fine by the time we went to school, but I can see it now. She's going to humiliate me in front of my friends. I'm going to spend the entire school year holding my breath, waiting for her next embarrassing incident.*

Back in their room, Caroline hung up her clothes and brushed her hair without giving any sign that she knew Chrissy was in the room. At last Chrissy could stand it no longer.

"Look, I'm sorry I embarrassed you this evening," she said. "But I don't know why you're so mad at me. It's only me they laughed at. I'm the only one they thought was a dummy."

"They turned around and looked at *us*, Chrissy," Caroline said coldly. "I do not happen to like strangers staring at me. I *liked* my life before you got here. I knew where I was and what I was doing, and I didn't keep getting mixed up in crazy situations."

"What crazy situations?" Chrissy asked.

"*What crazy situations?*" Caroline's voice rose to a squeak. "You don't think riding home in fire trucks is crazy or illegally wading in a public park or wrestling with a couple of punks?"

"What would you have done? Gone for a ride on their bikes with them?"

"Of course not! I would have talked calmly to them until I made them see that I was not interested. Then I would have calmly walked home."

"Oh, sure. They looked like they were about to take no for an answer when I gave that guy a good shove."

"So maybe that time it was a good thing you don't mind messing with strangers," Caroline said, sitting down on her bed and brushing out her hair fiercely. "But it's every day, Chrissy. You have to talk to everyone you meet. It embarrasses the heck out of me when you start chatting with people we've never seen before. We don't behave like that in cities."

For a few moments, the stroking of Caroline's brush made the only sound. Then Chrissy spoke. "Are you, by any chance, mad that I spoke to Alex this afternoon?"

"Me? Mad? Why should I be? Were you saying anything to him you shouldn't have been?"

"I just get the feeling," Chrissy said evenly, "that all this anger about me speaking to strangers might have something to do with the fact that I was chatting with Alex when you came home."

"Is that what you call it? Chatting?" Caroline asked. "Is that what chatting with strangers is like back in Iowa?"

"I don't get you."

"I'm not blind, Chrissy. I saw you. You were sitting very close together and you were gazing at Alex and I heard him mention something about a date."

Chrissy looked at Caroline in amazement for a moment. Then a big grin spread across her face. "If you'd listened a little harder, you would have heard Alex say that I'd helped him with a problem, and that if I ever had a problem I'd like to talk about, he'd take me to his special pizza parlor. That was all."

"Problem?" Caroline asked. "What problem?"

"You," Chrissy said. "We talked about you. He thinks you never have time for him because of ballet."

"He told you that?" Caroline asked. Chrissy nodded. "He was upset when he came up here. He wanted to surprise you, but you weren't here. He thinks he doesn't matter much to you, Caroline. Ballet always seems to come first."

"Why didn't he ever tell me this?" Caroline asked suspiciously.

"Because he cares too much about you, I guess,"

Chrissy said. "He was scared if he forced you to choose between him and ballet lessons, you'd choose ballet."

"He's a dope," Caroline said, half laughing with relief. "As if I'd do that. I'm crazy about him, and I certainly don't want to lose him."

"Then make some more time for him," Chrissy said.

"But it's so hard," Caroline said with a sigh. "I've been accepted for the performing company this year. It means classes almost every day. It's a big honor, Chrissy. They only take twelve students every year. I could be accepted by one of the big ballet companies when I finish."

"Alex just needs to know that he's special to you," Chrissy said. "If you make a big effort for him, I'm sure he'd be more understanding about the ballet."

Caroline nodded. "You know, you're right. I have just sort of fitted him in when I had time. I've turned down parties and dates that must have been important to him. I'll let him know that I'll give him every moment I possibly can—maybe I'll even drag him along to my rehearsals sometimes."

Caroline looked up at Chrissy and smiled. Dropping her hairbrush, she walked over to sit down beside her cousin. "I'm sorry I was such an old grouch to you," she said. "I guess I *was* jealous and scared when I saw you and Alex together."

"You don't have to be jealous of me," Chrissy said. "I'm no threat to you. I have the greatest guy in the world waiting for me at home. I wouldn't even be interested if every movie star in California asked me out on a date!"

Caroline laughed. "It must be really hard for you to be apart from him," she said. Chrissy nodded.

"But I'm sure he'll wait for me," she said. "We small-town folks don't go flitting from boy to boy. My mom met my dad in seventh grade."

"So you think this might be it for you?" Caroline asked. "You really want to settle down right there in Iowa?"

"I don't know about that yet," Chrissy said. "After tonight I think it might be fun to be an opera singer!" She burst out laughing at Caroline's terrified face.

Eight

"That was Tracy on the phone," Caroline said, joining her mother and Chrissy at the breakfast table. She looked at the other two and beamed. "She and Justine just got back from Europe. They had a really exciting time. They even got invited by a count to stay in his villa. Imagine that! They actually went to the villa, only it turned out there were no other women there—just the count and his brother and the butler. They had to talk themselves out of it politely again. I wish I'd gone."

"Well, I don't," her mother said. "I'm very glad you didn't find yourself in such a worrisome situation."

"But it would have been an adventure, Mom. It would have been one of the things you remember all your life and tell your grandkids. A lot better than trudging around the Louvre Museum in Paris for ten hours straight."

"It was not ten hours straight, Caroline. You do exaggerate. And think of all the wonderful paintings you were exposed to."

"Mother, after three hours I could barely tell Mona Lisa from Whistler's Mother," Caroline said. "Anyway, Tracy and Justine skipped the Louvre this time and concentrated on eating in every bistro on the Left Bank. I can't wait to see their photos. They actually took pictures of themselves with the count, inside the villa, before they discovered the no-women situation! Tracy said he was a real babe."

"So are they coming around today?" her mother asked. "Or will they be sleeping off jet lag?"

Caroline grinned again. "Randy wants us all to go to the beach," she said. "It's supposed to get really hot today!"

"Oh, wow! I get to go to the beach at last," Chrissy broke in. "I was beginning to think the beach was only a myth!"

Caroline opened her mouth to speak and closed it again. She glanced across at Chrissy. In the excitement of talking to her friends again, she had completely forgotten Chrissy. She hadn't even told Tracy about Chrissy. Was she selfish to want her friends to herself? She was looking forward to catching up on all the gossip after a summer apart. She also wanted to prepare them for Chrissy before they finally met her.

She was trying to think up a reasonable excuse to be alone with the group when she caught sight of Chrissy's face. It was alight with excitement. Her eyes really sparkled, as if someone had turned on a switch.

"And I finally get to meet your friends," Chrissy went on, unaware of Caroline's internal struggle. Embarrassing moments with Chrissy flashed through her mind as she played at slicing a peach into her cereal.

"What a good idea," her mother was saying. "Chrissy will have the chance to meet everyone before school starts."

"I really don't know about today," Caroline said hesitantly. "I didn't check with the others. Tracy was sort of organizing the party. I'm not sure I can just bring someone along uninvited."

"Nonsense," Mrs. Kirby said brightly. "I'm sure they'll be delighted to meet Chrissy. And you know how she's been longing to go to the beach."

"I know that, Mom," Caroline began. "But I'm not even sure if there'll be room in the car for one more. Randy was phoning Dino to see if he could get the van. If he can't, we'll have to go in Randy's little car."

"But Chrissy doesn't take up much space," Caroline's mother said. "She's as skinny as you. Of course she'll come along. It will be a wonderful chance for her, and the weather will be perfect."

"It's okay, Aunt Edith," Chrissy said. The light had disappeared from her eyes. "If Caroline would rather be alone with her friends, I understand."

Caroline stared down at the slices of peach floating gently on the milk in her cereal bowl. "No, you can come," she said with effort. "I'm sure we can squeeze you in. You need to meet people before school starts."

"Oh, wow," Chrissy said again, jumping up and

creating a minor earthquake that made the peaches rock violently. "I'll go get ready. Will my bikini be right or should I wear my plain black one-piece?"

"Whichever," Caroline said. "Nobody cares what you wear, but you better bring plenty of sunscreen for the parts of you that aren't tanned enough yet."

Chrissy rushed to the bedroom. Caroline could hear drawers opening and slamming shut again. She suspected that Chrissy's bed would quickly be covered with a new pile of clothes. She got up. "I'd better go make us some lunch," she said. Her mother looked up with understanding.

"It's her first ocean beach ever, Cara," she said. "See how excited she is? Don't spoil it for her. When she makes friends of her own, you'll have your friends to yourself again."

Caroline managed a convincing smile. "It's okay, Mom," she said. "I just hope she doesn't meet a great white shark or get swept out to sea or something. Things do seem to happen to her!"

"I'm sure she'll be just fine," Mrs. Kirby said, as Caroline pushed away her half-eaten bowl of cereal. "I'm not too hungry this morning," she said, walking across to the refrigerator and taking out cheese and fruit. She threw the food and some sodas into the cooler bag, then went to get changed. Chrissy was still in the room, surrounded by half her wardrobe.

"Do you think I need a sweater in case it gets cold later?" she asked. "Is this bikini too little? I wouldn't want it to get washed away by a big wave."

"That will do fine," Caroline said, opening her own drawer slowly.

"You're sure?" Chrissy asked. "What are you going to wear? I don't want to look like a freak."

Caroline had not really decided what to wear. She had also bought a new, bright blue bikini for the summer, but she had never dared to wear it. *I guess I'll just wear my old one-piece*, she thought. *At least I feel safe in that.*

"Will Alex be coming, too?" Chrissy asked, holding one tank top after another up against herself and staring at the mirror. It was an innocent question, but Caroline looked at her suspiciously. Chrissy had been wearing the tiny bikini the first time Alex saw her. Chrissy had sworn that all they had done was talk about Alex and Caroline, but Caroline had seen Alex's eyes riveted to that bikini. Would she be asking for trouble if she wore the plain old one-piece and let Chrissy dazzle Alex again? *Stop being so suspicious!* She scolded herself. *Have a little confidence. It's you Alex likes; Chrissy has a boyfriend of her own. Don't worry about nothing!*

All the same, she took the new blue bikini out of her drawer and stuffed it into her bag. Chrissy still had not attempted to put away the avalanche of clothing when there was loud honking outside their window. Chrissy peeked out the window.

"Is it them?" Caroline asked, picking some of Chrissy's things off the floor and tossing them onto the bed.

"It's a van with surfers and waves and palm trees painted on the sides," Chrissy said in awe.

"Oh great, Dino got his brother's van. Now we won't be too scrunched," Caroline said, heading for the door.

"Is the van advertising something?" Chrissy asked.

Caroline laughed. "No, why should it be?"

"Those pictures on the sides," Chrissy said.

"Dino's brother is into surfing in a big way. Lots of the surfers have pictures painted on their cars and vans," Caroline said. "Haven't you ever seen that before?"

"No," Chrissy said. "The only van I've seen with pictures on its side belongs to our butcher. He has a big black-and-white cow."

"You do say funny things," Caroline said. She paused in the doorway. "Look, Chrissy," she said, hesitantly. "In front of my friends—just cool it, will you? I mean, don't make them think you're weird."

"Why would they think I'm weird?" Chrissy asked, looking hurt and angry at the same time. "Just because I ask about things I've never seen before."

"They just wouldn't understand, that's all," Caroline said. "They all travel a lot, and they take it for granted that everybody has seen everything. I just don't want them to laugh at you."

"Why should they laugh at me?" Chrissy asked, her eyes moist. "I wouldn't laugh at them if they came to our farm and didn't know a cow from a bull. I can't change the way I am, Caroline. I'm used to saying what I feel. When I'm excited, I have to let people know it. And I'm not ashamed to admit that something is new to me. In fact, I'm not ashamed of myself at all, although you obviously are."

"Hey, no, that's not true," Caroline said. "I'm not ashamed of you, Chrissy. It's just, well, I know my friends, that's all. They're real city kids. They're used to putting people down for fun. They have a very dry sense of humor. I don't want you to leave yourself open to any of their jokes."

Just then the horn sounded again, this time twice as loudly as before. Caroline didn't say any more. Chrissy followed her obediently down the stairs.

"Hi, Cara, hop on up," Maria called from the front seat of the van as the girls approached the street. Someone inside slid open the side door, and hands reached down to grab at Caroline and Chrissy.

"Hi, everyone," Caroline said shyly. "I hope you don't mind, but I brought my cousin Chrissy along. She's visiting from out of town."

"Well, I don't know if there's room for a second overweight person back here," Randy quipped from the backseat. "You already take up more than your share of room, Caroline."

"Don't you listen to a word he says," Maria called from the front, swiveling around to face Caroline and Chrissy. "He's been like that all morning. Tracy and I are going to hold his head under a big wave!" She focused on Chrissy and beamed at her. "Hi, Chrissy," she said. "Go sit next to Randy, and make him move over. He brought too much stuff with him as usual. And don't mind any of these people. I'm Maria, by the way, and this guy next to me is Dino. You'd better be nice to him because he's the driver."

Caroline helped Chrissy into the very back seat, then she slipped into the seat in front, and Tracy leaned over to hug her. "Caroline, it's so great to see you. You look fabulous." She turned to smile at Chrissy. "I'm Tracy," she said. "This is George. Welcome to California."

"Er, thank you," Chrissy mumbled. Caroline looked back in surprise. She had never seen Chrissy either shy or at a loss for words before. Caroline watched her gaze go from one person to the next.

"The two in the back beside you are Justine and Randy," Caroline told her kindly. "I'll leave you to judge which is which!"

"Thanks a lot, Cara," Randy said, laughing.

Justine smiled in a kind way at Chrissy. "I guess we're a bit overpowering to meet all at once," she said.

"Well, we do have such charismatic personalities," Randy said, smiling smoothly. "True San Francisco extroverts. Everyone gets a shock when they meet San Franciscans for the first time."

"I'll bet Chrissy thought we'd all be real weirdos," Maria said from the front seat.

"And we're not?" George asked. Everyone laughed. Caroline noticed that Chrissy didn't join in.

"So tell us, Chrissy, did you imagine from Caroline's descriptions that we'd be such a charming group?" Randy asked.

Chrissy shook her head. "I mean—you're all so different," she said.

"Different from what?" Justine asked with interest.

"I hope you mean from whom!" Randy added.

"From one another," Chrissy mumbled. "Caroline told me a lot about you all, but I guess I expected you all to be the same. You know, back home everyone's family is either from Germany or Scandinavia. All my friends are German or Swedish or Norwegian. I guess I wasn't prepared for Caroline's friends not to look like her."

Caroline shot Chrissy a horrified look. In her worst fantasies she hadn't imagined that Chrissy would start probing her friends' racial backgrounds.

"You mean we don't look alike?" Dino asked from the front seat in shocked tones. "I always thought Randy and I could pass for identical twins."

"I'll have you know my family came over with the Mayflower," Randy quipped back.

Dino laughed. "Yeah, I hear there were a few rats on that ship," he said. Everyone joined in the laughter.

"You'll have to forgive Chrissy, but she comes from a very small town," Caroline said hastily.

"That's really understandable," Tracy said, smiling at Chrissy. "I don't suppose you do get much of a racial mix outside of big cities. That's what makes San Francisco so nice. How long have you been here, Chrissy?"

"A couple of weeks," Chrissy said, smiling shyly at Tracy. "How long have you been here?"

Tracy looked surprised. "All my life," she said.

"Oh, I'm sorry," Chrissy stammered. "I thought maybe you'd come from China or somewhere."

Caroline stared out of the window, pretending once again to be occupied with the passing scenery, really dying of embarrassment. *It's happened just the way I thought it would,* she thought gloomily. *Chrissy's making a big fool of herself, and my friends all think she's the world's biggest weirdo.*

Tracy giggled. "My great-great-grandfather came

from China," she said. "He came over to help build the railroads. But most Chinese people in this city have been here quite a while. Most of us can't even speak Chinese any more."

"I can count to ten," George said.

"You, you're useless," Tracy said, pushing him playfully. "I can speak quite a bit because my grandmother lives with us and she always speaks Cantonese."

"Hey, that's very interesting," Chrissy said, leaning forward toward Tracy's seat. "I'd love to meet her sometime. I never met a real Chinese grandmother."

"You should meet my Italian grandmother if you want to see a real character," Maria interrupted. "She's this tiny little lady who always wears black. All her sons are terrified of her. When she's cooking, she throws pots and pans around like crazy."

"But she makes the world's best pasta," Justine said.

A clamor engulfed Caroline as everyone began comparing grandmothers' recipes. Chrissy's shyness seemed to have vanished as she described Grandma Hansen's Thanksgiving feast.

"Aren't grandmothers something?" Dino asked. "Whenever I run out of allowance money and my father starts lecturing me about financial responsibility, my grandma always sneaks a five into my pocket. I love those lectures. They're a great way to get money from my grandmother without even having to ask." The van rocked with laughter around Caroline.

"Poor Caroline," Chrissy said, turning to her cousin. "It must have been so hard for you to grow up with no family."

Caroline mumbled something while Chrissy launched into an explanation for the crowd. Caroline didn't listen. Her thoughts were tumbling over one another. How had it happened? How had Chrissy twisted things around so that suddenly she was in thick, and Caroline was once again the outsider?

Nine

The van crept to the top of one of the steepest hills in the city and came to a halt outside the familiar blue-and-white wooden house. Dino honked loudly. Alex emerged immediately. He slid back the side panel and climbed up beside Caroline, giving her a quick kiss before turning to grin at the others. Finally he turned to Chrissy.

"We meet again on another bikini occasion," he said.

"Have you two been beach-partying without us?" Maria asked, frowning at Alex.

"Beach-partying?" Alex demanded in a hurt voice. "I'll have you know that I have been trekking over snow-capped mountains with three hundred pounds on my back, sleeping on rocky cliff faces, and living on disgusting dried food. Most nights it was barely warm, lumpy beef stew and most mornings it was barely warm, lumpy scrambled eggs."

"Poor Alex," Tracy said, patting his leg. "You're not the only one who suffered. We had to live on foreign food for a whole month. Imagine, they don't even serve ketchup with the hamburgers at McDonald's in Paris!"

"You'll have to tell us all about Europe while we're barbequing," Maria said. "Frankly, I'm green with envy."

"I don't see what you've got to be envious about," Tracy said. "I don't think that a whole summer with a stinking rich family in Mexico is too much of a hardship."

"I survived." Maria grinned.

"So how was your summer, Cara?" Justine asked.

"Pretty boring until Chrissy showed up," Caroline heard herself admit.

"Oh, really?" Justine asked, looking at Chrissy with interest. "What fun things have you done since she got here?"

Caroline opened her mouth to talk about the day in the park, or the bag lady, or Chrissy's arrival by fire truck, but she stopped as she looked from Maria's expectant face to Justine's to Tracy's. People who had been to Mexico and France would probably find those episodes silly and juvenile.

"Oh, we've just been shopping and done the usual sightseeing things, I guess," Caroline said. "But it's fun with someone who's never been here before."

"We've had such adventures," Chrissy said excitedly. Caroline prayed she wouldn't describe any of the more embarrassing ones.

"Really?" Justine asked. "I must say I've never thought of San Francisco as an adventurous type of place. Now Rome, for example, things happen to you in Rome."

"Like meeting Italian counts?" Randy quipped.

"Naturally, that was one of the minor adventures," Justine said calmly. "He was *very* good-looking. A little like you, Randall." She leaned across and lovingly touched his cheek.

"So when did you get back, *Randall?*" Alex asked, leaning across Caroline and Chrissy to talk to him.

"Last week. We had a terrific time."

"Where were you, Randy?" Caroline asked.

"In Sydney, mostly," he said.

"Oh, you were in Sidney?" Chrissy asked excitedly. "I've been there."

"Really?" Randy asked, surprised.

"Oh, sure," Chrissy went on. Caroline waited to see what Chrissy would say next. She had never mentioned a trip to Australia before. "Were you there for the rodeo?"

"Rodeo?" Randy sounded really confused. "I didn't know there was one."

"Oh, yes, it's a big one, in August."

"I didn't know that. I was there for the yacht races."

"Yacht races?" Chrissy asked. "I didn't know there was any lake nearby. Where do they sail?"

"From the harbor," Randy said. "Where else?"

There was a pause. "Are we talking about the same Sidney?" Chrissy asked in a small voice. "I was thinking of Sidney, Iowa."

"Sidney, Iowa?" Randy laughed. "I didn't even

know there was a Sidney, Iowa. I was in Sydney, Australia!"

"Oh. Sydney, Australia," Chrissy said, her face flushing red. "I never met anyone who'd been all the way to Australia before." There was a brief silence, then Chrissy burst out laughing. "You must have thought you had a complete weirdo in the car with you." She giggled. "Especially when I asked you about the rodeo! Do you think Australians have kangaroo rodeos?"

Caroline shot her a quick, embarrassed glance. "Chrissy hasn't ever traveled before," she said quickly. "You'll have to excuse her lack of knowledge about the rest of the world."

"That's okay," Randy said. "I thought it was pretty funny. And I've never been to Sidney, Iowa, so that makes us even. Tell me about Sidney, Iowa, Chrissy. Maybe I missed the best Sydney!"

Caroline tried to turn her attention to the boats on the bay while Chrissy described the rodeo and how her boyfriend had won the calf-roping event one year. *They'll all tease me about Chrissy later*, she thought. *How can she say such dumb things over and over again?*

"Holy cow!" Chrissy suddenly shouted in a voice that threatened to split Caroline's eardrums. "This really is it! This is the Golden Gate Bridge. Gee, it's bigger than it looks on TV. Look at those tiny boats way down there. It's just like being in a plane again."

"You wait until we drive over Mount Tam," Alex said to her. "Then you'll really get a good view of the Bay from high up."

"This is so exciting," Chrissy said, perched on the

edge of her seat and twisting to look first out one window, then the other. "Back where I come from, they call the greens on the golf course hills! I'm driving up a real mountain for the first time in my life."

"Mount Tam is just a small mountain," Maria said in a kindly way, turning to smile at Chrissy. "You should come up to the Sierra with us if you want real mountains. My folks have a cabin up at Lake Tahoe, in Nevada. That's six thousand feet high, and the mountains have snow on them all year."

"Oh, wow," Chrissy said again for what Caroline was sure was the hundredth time that morning.

The bridge was behind them now, the road had started to curve in a series of hairpin turns over the flanks of the mountain. Fragrant trees shaded the road in places, throwing patches of deep shadow onto the bright surface. On one side of the van, the land fell away sharply into a series of steep ravines. Through the gaps in the trees, the white buildings of San Francisco rose in the distance.

"I can't wait to see the ocean," Chrissy said, now bouncing around in her seat like a jack-in-the-box, to peer at the changing view as the van went higher and higher. "There's so much to see, it's hard to look at everything at once," she said as the road continued to climb among the golden meadows above the trees.

"You'll get your first glimpse of the Pacific soon," Tracy said to Chrissy. "We'll have a perfect view. There's no fog today."

Caroline noticed that Chrissy suddenly was no longer bouncing.

"Sorry, you guys," Chrissy said a moment later in a

subdued voice. "But I think I might be the sort of person who gets car sick."

"That's okay, Chrissy. Don't worry about it," Maria said.

Caroline said nothing. *If they think it's going to be like having a kid sister along every time we go anywhere from now on, I'm going to stop getting invited really fast,* she thought.

Caroline stared silently out the window, until the road finally reached its crest and began to descend again in another series of loops. The shining Pacific Ocean drew nearer. At last they turned into the sandy asphalt parking area beside the beach, and everyone tumbled out as soon as Dino had cut the engine.

Chrissy revived instantly when she saw the beach. "Oh, look at that," she called, jumping down from the van and racing ahead of the others toward the golden sand. "It's just the way I imagined it. Sand and waves and seashells—it's just perfect!"

She stopped to pull off her shoes and wiggled her toes in the sand. Alex took Caroline's hand and pulled her over to join Chrissy.

"Do you mean you've never been on a beach before?" he asked.

Chrissy shook her head. "Never, unless you count a few old lakes. But lakes don't have waves like these breaking on them. Listen to the sound they make. And it smells so good here. Nice and clean!"

"You're right, it does," Alex agreed. "It's funny how much you take for granted. I never noticed the ocean had a special smell."

They walked together to the water's edge.

"Are you coming surfing, Alex?" Dino called.

"You want to try surfing?" Alex asked Chrissy.

"No, thanks. I'd better just stand here near the edge until I get used to oceans," she said with a grin. "I'm not the world's greatest swimmer, you know. In fact, I can doggy paddle, but that's about all."

"Are you coming to get changed, Chrissy?" Tracy called. "There are changing rooms back beyond the dunes."

"I'll be there in a minute," Chrissy yelled back. "I just want to feel an ocean first!"

"Coming, Cara?" Tracy called.

"I'll join you guys in a little while," Caroline called back, not wanting to leave a self-confessed doggy paddler alone at the edge of the ocean. "You go ahead."

Tracy, Maria, and Justine walked toward the changing rooms. The boys were unloading surf boards from the van. Caroline stood on the sand watching Chrissy as she stepped carefully into the foamy surf, holding her shoes in one hand. She turned back to Caroline and made a pained face. "It's freezing!" she yelled. But she walked into the deeper water anyway.

Caroline shook her head as she watched Chrissy advancing and retreating with the tide as a little kid might. *She doesn't care at all what sort of image she projects*, Caroline thought.

What am I going to do with her? she wondered. *Will I ever stop feeling responsible for her? I feel like I'm on permanent baby-sitting duty. I wonder if the others are laughing about her, in the bathroom. I bet they think she's really weird. I could have died when she said all those dumb things in the car. Sidney, Iowa! I bet they're having a good laugh over that. I don't know how I'm going to get through a whole school year. I'll be known as Caroline Kirby, Chrissy Madden's poor cousin.*

A small wave swept past Chrissy before she could run away and wet the bottoms of her shorts. Chrissy yelled half in fear, half in delight.

"Watch out for the big waves," Caroline yelled to her. *I sound like a kindergarten teacher,* she thought gloomily. *To think that while Tracy and Justine were choosing another bistro on the Left Bank of Paris, I was stopping Chrissy from climbing on luggage carousels and watching her wade around the park with toy boats.*

Chrissy turned back to Caroline again. "If I started swimming," she yelled, "I could keep going until I got to Asia! Only I can't swim that far. If we had a big enough telescope we could take a peek at the people in Japan right now!" She laughed as she spoke. Caroline had to smile at Chrissy's unself-conscious pleasure.

"You dumbo," she called back. "What about the curve of the Earth?" Then she froze. A large wave was racing toward Chrissy, who had turned her back to the tide.

"Chrissy," Caroline yelled. "Watch out!"

Chrissy half turned, then began to make for the shore. The wave broke with a roar and a thump right behind her. It seemed to pull her off her feet, and she quickly disappeared into the rushing foam.

"Chrissy!" Caroline screamed again, racing toward the edge of the ocean. Caroline's heart was pounding as she ran down the beach. The soft sand slowed her unbearably. She imagined going home without Chrissy, telling her mother that she had been swept away by her first ocean wave. She scanned the ocean for a sign of Chrissy's red shirt. If Chrissy had been unlucky enough to meet a riptide, she could have been out beyond the waves by now. Caroline was also not the world's greatest swimmer, but she was not going to stop going until Chrissy was safe on shore.

But the boys also saw that something was wrong.

"What happened?" Alex yelled, running toward Caroline.

"A big wave broke over Chrissy. I can't see her!" Caroline screamed.

Alex and George overtook her with giant strides. Before they reached the ocean, a wave deposited Chrissy in a limp, sandy bundle at the top of the surf. They rushed to her. Caroline could only stand like a statue. She felt that her heart might leap right out of her throat at any moment. It wasn't real—she was just watching a movie—a movie in slow motion: boys running in huge, slow strides, the wave receding, Chrissy lying motionless like a bundle of rags at the water's edge.

She started to run again, staggering over the soft sand to the water. Alex had dragged Chrissy clear of the tide. Caroline dropped to her knees beside her cousin.

"Chrissy?" she whispered.

The limp, sandy bundle uncurled, coughed, looked up at them, and managed a feeble grin.

"I just learned something about oceans," she said,

sitting up and still panting as she spoke. "I just learned that oceans don't stay where they are. They come and get you."

The others laughed in relief. "We'd better get you away from here before another wave comes for you," Alex said. "You gave us a real scare, Chrissy."

"Gave *you* a scare?" Chrissy asked, rising cautiously to her feet. "What about me? Holy Toledo, was that a shock! I half expected to open my eyes and find myself in Tokyo!"

Only a few minutes later, Chrissy, dressed in Caroline's jacket, Tracy's shorts, and Maria's spare T-shirt, was eating roasted hot dogs as if nothing very unusual had happened to her.

Caroline was still trembling with fright. "I don't think she realizes how close she came to drowning," Caroline said to Alex, as they walked down the beach together. "If she'd have hit a rip, we'd never have found her."

Alex nodded. "She's a gutsy girl, your cousin," he said. "The guys all think she's terrific. She didn't cry or make any fuss at all. Most girls would have had hysterics."

"They would not, Alex. You are prejudiced," Caroline said.

"All right, let me rephrase that," Alex said with a good-natured grin. "Most *people* would have panicked if they were hit by a giant wave their first time at the beach. Is that correct?"

"I guess so," Caroline said.

"So she's a pretty gutsy kid," Alex repeated. "And she's fun, too. I'm glad you brought her along."

Caroline grinned up at him. "You know what, Alex? So am I. I can't exactly say she's the easiest person in the world to get along with, but I realized while I was standing there on the beach that I really would miss her if she weren't around any more."

Still, Caroline was shocked to hear Maria and Tracy repeat nearly the same thing later as the girls were changing back to street clothes.

"I really like your cousin," Maria said. "She's fun."

"You do?" Caroline asked.

"Yeah," Tracy agreed. "She's a nice girl—and brave, too. I would have been scared to death if it had happened to me. I would have wanted to go home right away and spoiled everyone else's day."

"She *was* pretty cool about the whole thing," Caroline admitted. "But she does say the most embarrassing things, doesn't she?"

"Like what?" Maria asked. "She's funny. That whole business with Sidney and Sydney was a laugh. She thought so, too. You're lucky to have a nice cousin, Cara. I'll trade you for one of mine—they're all obnoxious, spoiled brats."

"You don't think she's a total hick?" Caroline ventured.

"A hick?" Maria asked. "Of course not. I think she fits in really well. She's smart and easy to talk to."

Caroline was amazed. Her friends actually liked Chrissy. They admired her. They thought her bubbling enthusiasm was fun, not naive. Caroline actually found herself confessing with pleasure about wading across the pond to get a little boy's boat, the park keeper who had chased them with his rake and Chrissy's arrival in the fire truck.

I should learn to trust my own feelings more, she thought as they rode home in the glowing pink twilight. *If I like her, why shouldn't my friends like her? Chrissy is right to say what she feels. People respect her for it, and they actually enjoy meeting someone who's not just like them! Now if only the rest of Maxwell High were as open-minded as her best friends.*

Ten

"Holy cow!" Chrissy said, flinging up her arms and grabbing onto Caroline so violently that they both nearly fell back down the concrete steps.

"What's the matter?" Caroline nervously asked. Her own stomach was already full of the usual first day of school butterflies. When Chrissy grabbed her, the butterflies turned into seven-forty-sevens.

"Look at all these people!" Chrissy hissed. "They don't all go to school here, do they?"

"I guess so, or they wouldn't be going up the steps ahead of us," Caroline said. "It's a big school, Chrissy. It takes awhile to get used to it."

"But I've never even been in a crowd this big before," Chrissy said, still clutching at Caroline as if she were a life-line. "Not even when I went to see the state football championships. I don't think there are this many people in the whole state of Iowa!"

The crowd of students closed around them as they approached the heavy double doors of the main entrance to Maxwell High. Once they were inside, the crowd swept them along.

"It's a good thing I wrestled with that wave," Chrissy yelled over the echoing din of voices, "or I might have panicked by now. What happens if you want to go the other way?"

"You don't," Caroline yelled back. "You just keep on going around the square, and eventually you'll get back to where you started."

"This place is like a jail!" Chrissy commented as they moved down the hall. "Why do they need bars on the windows? To keep students in or to keep other people out? What's that policeman doing here?"

"He's only a security guard. They have one on each hall."

"What for?"

"To break up fights."

"Fights? What sort of fights? You mean we're in danger just walking down the halls here? I didn't come to California to be stabbed."

I wish she'd be quiet for a minute, Caroline thought, glancing through the crowd for signs of a familiar face. *Doesn't she realize that I'm nervous about my first day back at school? I wish I could see someone I know.*

"I hope you can find me again at the end of the day," Chrissy said. "I'd hate to have to spend an entire year stuck in this building looking for the way out."

"It's not that bad," Caroline said. "Remember what

I said about the building being a square. If you keep walking long enough, you get back to where you started."

"I hope we get lots of classes together," Chrissy said. "I hope I can find my way to classes in time, and they don't yell at me. I hope I know somebody. I hope my records have arrived from Danbury. I hope the classes aren't too hard . . ."

"Relax. You'll do fine," Caroline said. "Mr. Weiss is a nice counselor. He'll make sure you get into good courses. Come on, this is the way to the administration hall."

She grabbed Chrissy's hand and pulled her out of the main tide of traffic into a quiet side-stream. Chrissy heaved a sigh of relief. "Phew!" she said, pushing back her hair from her face. "So many strangers all at once. I don't recognize a single face so far. I hope I don't go all year without making one friend."

"Don't worry, you'll meet plenty of people," Caroline said. "I'll introduce you to more of my friends at lunchtime. You've already made friends with my best friends . . ." Caroline followed Chrissy's fascinated glance toward the guidance counselors' offices.

A group of girls was coming out of the office toward Caroline and Chrissy. It was Dolores Wright and her gang of admirers. Tall, blond Dolores was dressed in a gray jump suit which showed off her perfect body. Her hair was short and sleek, her face perfectly made up. Princess Di, some of the boys called her. Her ladies-in-waiting were only slightly less beautiful and just as well dressed.

"Hey, Cara," Chrissy whispered. "Who are those

girls? They look like models. *Are* they models? Look how everything matches—their shoes and their purses and even their jewelry."

Caroline glanced across at the group of girls, hoping they hadn't heard Chrissy's whispers. "That's—" she began, but before she could go on, Dolores noticed her.

"Hey, Cara. How are you? How was your summer?" she drawled, as if whatever Caroline had to say wouldn't be particularly interesting.

"Pretty good. Thanks, Dolores," Caroline muttered. "How about you?"

"Club Med, darling," Dolores cooed. "All those French hunks in tiny swimsuits. Gorgeous."

"Sounds great," Caroline said. "We stayed home because my mother was away in Iowa. Then my cousin from Iowa came here to spend the year."

"Is this her?" Dolores asked, looking at Chrissy as if she were a museum specimen.

"That's right. Dolores, I'd like you to meet my cousin Chrissy. Chrissy, this is Dolores."

"Hi, sweetie," Dolores said. She turned back to Caroline. "You've got to come over and see my birthday present," she said breathily. "It's the dearest, sweetest little poodle puppy you've ever seen. He's like a cotton puff, all white and fluffy and round. And he's so smart. When he wants to go out, he goes and presses his little nose up against the door and just stands there like that until someone opens it for him. Isn't that cute?"

"Hey, that's amazing," Chrissy said. "I used to have a piglet that did the same thing."

Several pairs of eyes turned to her.

"You what?" Dolores asked, shaking her head as if she hadn't heard right.

"My little hog used to do exactly the same thing."

"You kept a hog in the house?" one of the girls asked suspiciously.

"He was very little at the time, but he was house-broken," Chrissy said enthusiastically. "Hogs are as smart as dogs are."

"Are we talking about the same sort of hogs?" Dolores asked. "They're big and pink, and you turn them into bacon?"

"That's them," Chrissy said, smiling at Dolores. "I used to get the runt of the litter to hand rear. They make good pets."

Caroline was conscious of the girls looking first at Chrissy and then at her. Their eyes asked clearly, "Where did you find this strange person?"

Dolores laughed uneasily. "Then maybe I'd better trade in my poodle for a hog," she said. She turned to her friends. "Come on, you guys, we'll be late for PE signups." They hurried off. Caroline wanted to tell Chrissy that talking about pet hogs was probably the last way to make friends with girls like Dolores Wright, but she couldn't find the words to say it. Poor Chrissy obviously hadn't realized she'd said anything dumb. Besides it was kind of funny to see the look on Dolores's face when Chrissy had compared her new poodle to a pig.

This thought was cut short by Chrissy leaping ahead of her down the hall.

"Hey, Chrissy. Where are you going?" Caroline

called, breaking into a run to catch up with her cousin. "The counselors' offices are this way!"

"Be right with you, Cara," Chrissy called, turning back to her cousin for a second. "I just saw someone I've got to talk to." She sprinted ahead. Caroline followed her, totally mystified. Who could Chrissy possibly know around the school? Caroline didn't recognize any of her own friends in the long hallway, and Chrissy hadn't had a chance to meet anyone else. The only guys Chrissy hadn't passed yet were some members of the football team, all wearing their numbered shirts as they did the first day of every year.

To Caroline's horror, she saw Chrissy draw level with Marvin Jones, huge linebacker and captain of the team. Hurrying to keep up with his huge stride, Chrissy tapped him on the arm. Caroline saw Marvin stop and look down at Chrissy. She was too far away to hear the conversation, but she saw his stony face break a little awkwardly into a smile as Chrissy continued an animated speech. Chrissy waved her arms as she spoke, then stopped, waved good-bye to Marvin, and ran back to Caroline again.

"He was a sweetie pie," she said as she joined Caroline.

"Would you mind explaining what that was about?" Caroline asked. "How on earth do you know Marvin?"

Chrissy turned her big, innocent eyes on Caroline. "Oh, is that his name?" she asked.

"Marvin Jones," Caroline said dryly. "Senior and captain of the football team and just about the best-known guy in this school."

"No kidding!" Chrissy said. "I have to write to Ben and tell him right away! He'll be tickled to hear that."

"Does Marvin know Ben?" Caroline asked, more confused then ever.

"Of course not," Chrissy said. "It's just that his number is the same. Good old number fifty-eight. It made me so homesick to see a shirt with the same number as Ben's on it. It's even yellow and black like the Danbury Hornets shirt. I just had to go tell the guy that he had the same number as my boyfriend!"

Caroline stared at her cousin. "You went up to the captain of our football team—a guy who weighs three hundred pounds—just to tell him that he has the same number on his shirt as your boyfriend?" she stammered.

"That's right," Chrissy said happily. "I feel much better now knowing that there's a good old number fifty-eight floating around school!"

Caroline shook her head in disbelief. "Come on," she said, glancing up at the clock on the wall. "We'd better hurry. I have my own classes to get to after I leave you with Mr. Weiss."

"Sorry if I made you late," Chrissy said quietly. "I guess it's hard for you to understand how I was feeling. Everything seemed so strange and scary in this great big building that when I caught a glimpse of something I recognized, I just had to run up to the guy and talk to him."

"It's okay, Chrissy," Caroline said. "I do understand. "It's just that things are different in a big school like this. You can't know everybody, so you just keep to your own little groups. And you don't usually go around grabbing strange guys in halls, especially if the strange guy happens to be the captain of the football team."

Chrissy grinned sheepishly. "Oh well," she said, flinging out her hands in a gesture of embarrassment. "Nothing like starting at the top, is there? You'd better promise to keep an eye on me, Cara, and make sure I don't act too weird too often."

"I'll try," Caroline said. She pointed to a doorway. "It's in through there. One of the secretaries will show you which desk is Mr. Weiss's. Good luck. I'll see you under that big clock in the front hall at lunchtime, and then we'll eat together, okay?"

"Okay, Cara," Chrissy said. "I haven't felt this way since my first day at kindergarten. When my mom walked away I ran after her and hung on to her leg. I'm tempted to grab your leg now."

"And wrinkle my skirt? Thanks a lot. I'm sorry, Chrissy, but I really have to go," Caroline said with sympathy. She really knew exactly how Chrissy felt. She had done exactly the same thing on her first day at kindergarten. Only she still felt like a new kindergartner on her first day at school every year, which was one of the reasons she didn't want to be late. Just the thought of being the last one to enter a full classroom, having to squeeze past everybody and take a seat next to the class nerd or creep turned her knees to jelly.

"Bye, Cara," Chrissy said softly. "Don't worry. I'm sure I'll be fine. I'll see you under the clock, if I can ever find the clock. I'm sure I'll find it, so don't worry. I'm sorry I can't seem to stop talking, but I always do that when I'm nervous. I guess I must be scared silly. Bye." She turned and waved before she disappeared through the doorway. Caroline turned and hurried to her own class. *How is it that every time I think I've got this situation figured out, Chrissy does something else that takes me by surprise?* Caroline wondered as she ran up the stairs. *I have a feeling this is still just the beginning of a very crazy year.*

Eleven

"What's wrong, Cara?" Maria asked as they stood together in the girls' bathroom the next day while Maria brushed through her thick black curls. "You've been so quiet today, even for you—and that's saying a lot. Don't you feel good, or have you just got the back-to-school blues?"

"I feel fine," Caroline said, staring at her own face in the mirror. She could see two parallel frown lines on her forehead. She tried to relax them away, but each time she checked the mirror, they had reappeared. "And I even like getting back to school. In fact, nothing's wrong, really," she said hesitantly.

"So you usually walk around like a zombie scowling at everyone?" Maria quipped. "Come on, Cara. Open up. Something's bugging you."

"Not really bugging me," Caroline began. "It's

Chrissy—but she's not bugging me. It's just that today it really hit me that I'm stuck with her all year. It's not that I don't like her, Maria—you just can't help liking Chrissy—it's just that I'm not used to having *anyone* around me all the time, and it's making me tense."

Caroline took the combs out of her hair and shook it out into a loose cascade around her face.

"But I thought you two were getting along fine," Maria said, grimacing as she tugged at a tangle. "I swear, birds build nests in my hair when I'm not looking!"

"We do get along fine," Caroline admitted, drawing a brush easily through her own fine hair. "And I thought things were going pretty well. She was getting really independent and seemed to like going off on her own around town. But we got to school yesterday, and she started clinging to me all over again. I mean, I could understand it. She comes from a school with three hundred people, all of whom know one another, and suddenly—wham!—Maxwell High with three thousand strangers. But I'm scared I'm going to get stuck with her as my sidekick all year, and I don't know if I could take that."

"She'll make some friends of her own soon," Maria said.

"I hope so," Caroline said, "I want her to fit in eventually, but she's so different from most people here. She still says the most embarrassing things. I met Dolores and her clique on the stairs yesterday, and I introduced Chrissy to them. Dolores was in the middle of a story about her new poodle puppy when Chrissy pipes up, Oh, I used to have a hog who did that!"

Maria burst out laughing. Caroline scowled at her. "It's not funny, Maria. I nearly died. All those girls stared at Chrissy and then looked at me as if I were responsible for her. Chrissy didn't seem to notice she was saying anything weird, and she went on to tell them how she hand rears and housetrains baby pigs. I ask you, Maria, is that normal conversation?"

Maria was still laughing so hard she could no longer brush her hair. "I think it's pretty funny," she said. "And Dolores is so stuck up. I can just see the way her face must have looked when Chrissy compared her new pedigreed puppy to a hog."

Even Caroline had to smile at the recollection of Dolores's expression. "I guess it was funny," she said. "But Chrissy will never be accepted here if she goes around saying stuff like that to everyone. And if she doesn't make some friends pretty quickly, I'm going to be a nervous wreck worrying what she'll say next. She actually stopped the captain of the football team in the hall yesterday—"

"Marvin?" Maria asked in amazement. "She stopped Marvin Jones in the hall. What for?"

Caroline wound her hair back into a knot and secured it with a comb. "She saw the number on his football shirt, and she had to tell him that was her boyfriend's number, too."

"Well, at least she's got guts," Maria said. "Going up and speaking to a strange three-hundred-pound boy!"

Caroline shook her head in disbelief. "I'd never have the nerve to talk to any senior I didn't know, even if he was in one of my classes."

Maria grinned at her friend. "Yes, well, we know about you," she said. "Until last year you hid in a closet every time *anyone* spoke to you."

"I did not!"

"Caroline Kirby, don't forget that I have been your friend since first grade. Even in elementary school, you'd jump a mile straight up if someone even said 'boo' to you. And have you forgotten that we had to walk around the block four times before you'd come into this school the first day of freshman year?"

"So—I'm naturally shy. I know that," Caroline said. "But I'm not shy to the point of being a weirdo. I never actually hid in a closet!"

"Well, you might as well have," Maria said. "If you hadn't gotten so worked up about that petition for those old houses, you'd have gone through high school unknown. That did wonders for your image."

"That's just it, Maria," Caroline said. "Just when I'm known around school as an okay person, I get stuck with a cousin who talks about housetrained hogs. I tell you, Maria, I'm doomed."

Maria put her hand on her friend's arm. "Don't worry so much. You know Chrissy's a total extrovert. Give her two weeks, and she'll know the entire school."

"I think you mean the entire school will know her," Caroline said grimly. "And I'm not so sure that will be a good thing. Come on, I promised to take her up to the Nob Hill Garden for lunch."

Chrissy was standing under the clock as Maria and Caroline came out of the bathroom. She peered through the crowd, her big blue eyes opened wide to search the tide of strangers sweeping past her for her cousin. She looked smaller and more lost and helpless than Caroline had known she could. Caroline instantly felt guilty that she had complained about being stuck with her cousin. Of course even Chrissy needed help settling into a big school like Maxwell. Caroline would have been completely helpless if her parents had shipped her off to a new city for an entire year. *Maybe she will change once she's used to being here*, Caroline thought hopefully as she walked toward the clock. *If I can learn not to hide out, maybe Chrissy can learn not to talk about the habits of pigs*.

"Hi," Caroline called out cheerfully, when she was close enough for Chrissy to hear. "How was your morning? Did you find your classes okay today?"

"It went fine, thanks," Chrissy said, her face full of delight to see Caroline. "I tied a string to Mr. Weiss's office door so I could find my way back and start again if I got lost." Caroline gaped at her in wordless horror. The delight in Chrissy's face turned to laughter. "Just kidding," she said. "You didn't really think I'd walk around school unraveling a string, did you?"

"Of course not," Caroline said hurriedly, turning her face so Chrissy wouldn't see its color. She scowled at Maria, whose brown eyes sparkled above a grin she was trying to bite back. "Come on, the others are waiting. We'll go up to our little park today. It's really private and quiet."

"Great," Chrissy said, swinging into step beside Caroline and Maria. "I thought my head was going to explode with the noise in that courtyard yesterday. I felt totally trapped. I'm used to looking out of the windows at school and seeing the fields. And I really miss being able to escape in the middle of the day. Doesn't anyone go home?"

Caroline shook her head. "We're officially not supposed to leave campus," she said. "And there wouldn't be time to get most places. They let us go to the parks nearby because if everybody followed the rules, the cafeteria and courtyard would be overcrowded."

"Did you go home for lunch?" Maria asked Chrissy. "I thought you lived way out on a farm."

"I didn't go to my house, I used to go to my grandma's," Chrissy explained. "She lives right across from the high school and she always cooked my brothers and me a hot lunch."

"Wow," Maria said. "Imagine that. If I could only have some of my Nonna's ravioli . . ." She closed her eyes and slowly licked her lips.

"You'd be as fat as a pig," Caroline quipped, laughing.

Maria chuckled and waved as she saw Tracy, Randy, Justine, and Alex waiting for them by the back door to the school building.

"How was your Spanish class today?" Tracy asked Chrissy. "A little less horrible than yesterday?"

Chrissy grinned. "It was fine," she said. "Only it was a little boring in just one foreign language instead of two."

"What are you talking about?" Caroline asked. "I didn't hear anything about Spanish class."

Tracy looked at Chrissy and smiled. "It was nothing," she said. "Just a private joke."

"No, it's okay. You can tell it," Chrissy said. "It *was* pretty funny."

Tracy turned to the others. "Chrissy came into my class and sat down yesterday. Instead of calling roll, the teacher made a seating chart and took everyone's name. About halfway through the period the teacher finally started talking about Paris and the Parisian accent. Then Chrissy blurted out, I thought Paris was in France. You can imagine the effect that had."

"But Paris *is* in France," Caroline said, confused. "I don't get it."

"I was in a French class by mistake!" Chrissy said, giggling. "I didn't know either language, so I didn't know I should have been next door until they talked about Paris. You should have seen the instructor's face!"

The group had walked out the back exit and across the parking lot and playing fields as they talked. Now they climbed the steep hill that separated the campus from the surrounding neighborhood and led to the small, landscaped lot between two white apartment buildings that faced a quiet side street.

"Here we are," Caroline said. "Peace and quiet. I wonder if the magnolias are in bloom. They are so . . ."

She broke off in mid-sentence. "What on earth?" she asked.

A yellow tape was stretched across the entrance to the park. "What's this for?" she demanded.

"Looks like it's to keep people like us out," Randy suggested.

"But why?" Caroline asked. She was about to duck under the tape when an elderly woman walked past with her dog. "The park's closed, honey," she said.

"They don't want you in there anymore because they've already started digging."

"Digging what?" Justine asked.

"Didn't you hear?" the woman asked, looking from one of them to the next. "They're going to build a multi-story parking garage here."

"A garage?" Caroline blurted out. "On the park? But they can't do that."

"I'm afraid they already have, honey," the old woman said with a sigh. "It's been through city council, and they've got planning permission and everything."

Caroline stared across the yellow tape at the sandy pathways, the broad magnolia trees, the graceful pines, and the bright green patches of grass. The aroma of flowers and moist earth drifted over the sidewalk. "Isn't anybody doing anything to stop it?" she asked.

The old woman shook her head. "What could anyone do?" she asked. "You can't fight these big conglomerates. They have too much money and too much political clout."

"But that's terrible," Caroline said. "Lots of people love this park. Somebody should do something to stop them."

"It's too late, honey," the old woman said with a tired smile. "They've already started staking the construction site. This park can't be saved."

She turned and began to shuffle on down the hill, the little brown dog straining at its leash.

"But that's awful," Chrissy exploded. "That's a crying shame. You ought to write up another petition, Cara."

"Oh, it sounds like it's too late for a petition," Caroline said hesitantly. "Anyway, I wasn't the real organizer. I just helped out."

"But you were good at it, Cara," Alex said, taking her hand. "You were the one who told people about it, and you were the one who demanded to talk to the mayor. For something like this park, I bet we could get a couple of thousand signatures at school alone. That would make them sit up at city hall!"

Caroline looked back at the doomed trees in the park. Fighting her shyness to plead with the mayor to save those houses was the most difficult thing she ever had done. She had hated asking people for signatures, hated seeing her picture in the newspaper, hated talking to the reporters, even on the phone. If she hadn't cared so much about the houses she never could have done any of it. *But you care just as much about this park,* a little voice in her head reminded her. *And Alex is right. You do know exactly what to do next.*

"I guess we could try," Caroline said, to a chorus of cheers from her friends. "We'd better meet at my house tonight and get a petition together. If we're going to do it, we've got to move fast. Those trees already have bands around them to be cut down."

"I'll help you, Cara," Chrissy said enthusiastically, squeezing her around the shoulders. "I'll do anything you want me to."

"Okay, Caroline Kirby, you're in charge," Maria said. "Chief protester and lobbyist for Maxwell High." A little chill skittered up Caroline's spine.

"Yeah, Cara," Tracy said. "After this you'll probably be asked to run for congress or something."

"More likely she'll be put on the city's Ten Most Wanted list," Randy said.

"Oh, stop it," Caroline said. She laughed uneasily. "I don't want you guys to think I like doing things like this. But we have to save this park, don't we?"

"Caroline Kirby, fighter for truth and justice," Justine said earnestly.

"She had greatness thrust upon her," Alex added.

"There comes a time in the lives of men and women and girls . . ." Maria said.

"I'm so excited, I can't think of anything, except *Four score and seven years ago . . .*" Chrissy said. "But I'm real proud of you, Cara, and I'm glad to help in any way I can."

Caroline smiled weakly. What had she promised to get herself into?

Twelve

"Now that we're here, I can't stop my knees from shaking," Chrissy said. "How about you guys?" Caroline, Alex, Tracy, George, Maria, Dino, Justine, Randy, and Chrissy had spent the evening and morning writing petitions and collecting signatures. They had raced to City Hall as soon as the lunch bell rang.

"I don't feel too great either," Maria admitted. "What about you, Cara?"

"Cara's already got her death-defying smile on her face," Randy said. "You know what she's like when she's fighting for a cause! Last summer we nicknamed her Iron Lady, Chrissy. Little things like talking to a planning commission don't even faze her, do they Cara?"

They were standing together in a tight little group on the steps of City Hall. Large, gray office buildings on all sides frowned onto the square behind them. Even though it was lunchtime, the fog had not cleared; the wind whipped between buildings as if it were mid-winter. Caroline shivered.

"Gee, it's cold today," she said. She looked around at the others. *Oh, why couldn't she come right out like Chrissy and admit that she was scared of going into City Hall? It was just too hard to do, after everyone had expressed so much confidence in her.*

She took a deep breath. "We'd better get on with this, or lunch will be over and we'll all be sitting in detention this afternoon."

"I think I'd rather face City Hall than the principal," Justine said. "I agree with Cara. Let's get it over with, or we'll all die of pneumonia before we even talk to the planning commission."

"Are you sure the appointment was for today?" Tracy asked. "We couldn't come back tomorrow maybe?"

"Come on, you guys," Alex said, moving close to Caroline. "Do we want to save this park or not? After all, we're dealing with humans in there. They can't do anything too horrible to us."

Caroline slipped her hand into Alex's and took a deep breath. "Let's go!" she said, smiling up at him.

With Caroline and Alex in the lead, the group marched down a cold, wide corridor until they reached the door marked, "Planning Department." With a quick glance at Alex for reassurance, Caroline grasped the cold, brass doorknob and turned it. She slowly pushed open the heavy, creaking door.

"Miss Hayward is expecting you," the girl behind

the desk said, as if she were explaining a very complicated problem to a very stupid group of young children. "I'll let her know you're here." She pushed a button on an intercom. "The high school students are here, Ms. Hayward," she said, watching them the whole time as if she expected one of them to walk off with her stapler.

"Send them right in," ordered the disembodied voice. The secretary jerked her head toward a closed door. "In there," she said and went back to her typing.

The woman behind the desk was a complete contrast to the secretary. She stood when the group came in and beamed at them as if they were favorite grandchildren she hadn't seen in years. "How good of you to come," she said. "I'm Marla Hayward of the planning commission. I hear you want to see me about a park?"

Caroline could feel herself being pushed forward. When she opened her mouth to speak, her throat felt so tight that she was sure no sound would come out. But she forced herself to say, in what she hoped was a calm, firm voice, "It's Nob Hill Gardens. Right up behind Maxwell High. They want to turn it into a parking lot."

Ms. Hayward rummaged in her files. "Nob Hill Gardens," she said. "Let me see . . . oh, here it is. Yes, that's right. Greater Bay Properties has received permission to construct a garage to service the residents of its condominium complex, on Taylor."

"Who could have given them permission?" Justine blurted. "People liked that park . . ."

For a fraction of a second Ms. Hayward's glance went cold. "They went through all the proper channels," she said crisply. "Their application was discussed and approved by the planning commission at a public hearing. You could have spoken up then."

"When was this meeting?" Caroline asked.

"Ms. Hayward consulted her notes again. "That would have been July eighteenth," she said. "At eight P.M."

"But we were out of school then," Tracy said angrily. "How could we have known about it? We only use the park when we're in school."

"We take our lunch up there," Maria added.

"I see," Ms. Hayward said. "I hadn't realized that students were allowed to leave school grounds during the day."

Caroline exchanged a quick glance with Alex. "The important things is, Ms. Hayward, that lots of people use that park. You are taking away public land to put in a parking garage for just a few privileged people. That doesn't sound fair, does it?"

Ms. Hayward smiled again. "You're quite right. It doesn't sound fair if it's put like that. But that's not the whole story. Bay Properties did a land swap with us. They had a large piece of land out near the ocean that they didn't want, and they donated that as a future park for the city. We'll have a much bigger, better park than that tiny little garden."

"But we won't be able to use it," Caroline said. "It's still taking a park away from the people of one neighborhood."

"The planning commission must think of the city as a whole," Ms. Hayward said. "The new park will benefit many more people."

Caroline opened her purse. "I have petitions with two thousand signatures from students and neighbors of the park," she said. "At least two thousand people want that park to be kept open."

Ms. Hayward looked impressed. "My, you have been busy, haven't you?" she said.

"We wanted to show you it wasn't just a few school kids," Caroline said. "It's the community. There must be some way to get the planning commission to reconsider, if it's what two thousand citizens want."

"Well, let me see," Ms. Hayward said carefully. "Why don't you leave your signatures with me and I'll present them at the commission meeting next week? They will certainly be taken into consideration. How does that sound?"

"That sounds okay," Caroline said hesitantly. "You really will show them to the commission?"

"Of course," Ms. Hayward said. "We will definitely consider them."

Caroline took a deep breath. "If the answer after your meeting is still no," Caroline went on, "we plan to show the petitions to the mayor and to the newspapers. We worked hard last year to keep a row of historical houses from being torn down, and we won then. We think we can win this time, too."

"I can see you are a very determined young woman," Ms. Hayward said, smiling at Caroline. "Just be patient and we'll do our best. Okay?"

"Thank you, Ms. Hayward," Caroline said. "Thank you," the others muttered after her. They turned and walked from the room.

"You see, what did I tell you?" Caroline squealed

when they were a safe distance from the planning office. "If you go about these things in an organized, adult way, they really do listen to you."

"I think the signatures really impressed her," Tracy said.

Caroline grinned. "Did you see the way her face changed when I mentioned newspapers?"

"You were great, Cara," Chrissy said. "They should rename the park the Caroline Kirby Memorial Park!"

"Hey, I don't intend to die for the cause just yet!" Caroline said, laughing with relief now that the meeting had ended.

"They'll put up a statue to you, Cara," Randy teased. "And mothers will stop as they push their babies in strollers. 'That was a famous lady who saved this park,' they'll tell them!"

"And pigeons will land on your head," Alex said.

As they walked back to school, Caroline privately replayed the scene in the office in her mind. "I see you are a very determined young woman," the commissioner had said.

I did it, Caroline said to herself in amazement. *I really did it. I talked to an important person, and I didn't stammer and stutter like a baby. I kept cool and she gave in. I didn't collapse under pressure. I'm not even shy when it really matters.*

A big grin spread across her face. The others had helped, but Caroline Kirby had been the leader.

"Hey look, guys," Tracy yelled, breaking into Caroline's thoughts. "We've got a welcoming committee! Maybe they'll carry us around the school on their shoulders like they do with the football team after a victory."

"I hope not," Justine said, horrified. "I have a skirt on today. So does Cara!"

Once again the group broke into laughing and wise-cracking as they approached the people lined up at the school entrance.

"Well, what do you know," Dino said. "The big stuff is out to greet us. Marvin Jones himself!"

Marvin and his football buddies had been sitting on the front steps. They stood up as the group approached, and Marvin called to them, "So I guess you didn't get in to see the city dudes."

"Yeah, what a drag after standing out in the cold to get those signatures this morning," Todd Jacobs agreed.

"We got in," Caroline said proudly, conscious that she was speaking directly to Marvin Jones for the first time in her life. "We saw the planning commissioner. She's agreed to take our petition to a member of the commission for consideration."

A grin spread over Marvin's face. "That's what she told you?" he demanded. He chuckled. "Yeah, that would make sense. She'll keep right on giving your petition nothing but consideration until that whole high rise lot is built!"

"Oh, no, Marvin," Chrissy said angrily. "She was no double-crosser. She listened to us. I believed her when she said she'd do something with those signatures."

"She was a good actress then," Marvin said. "I just

went up to your park, and there's a bulldozer out there right now." A hearty laugh rumbled out of him.

"What?" Caroline shrieked.

"And he looks like he means business," Todd added with a grin. "He looks like he wants to dig a great big hole today!"

"Why the slimy, double-crossing little—" Chrissy began.

"We'd better get up there right now," Alex suggested. "See what we can do to stop them. Maybe they just didn't get the order to stop yet."

"We'll come with you," Marvin said, turning to his buddies. "I'm just dying to see how you folks propose to stop a bulldozer!"

"I'm sure the driver will listen to reason and call City Hall before he does any damage," Caroline said.

A few minutes later, they arrived, panting, at the site, with a small audience not far behind. The tape was now down across the entrance. A huge yellow bulldozer was perched at the entrance; a man in a yellow hard-hat was just walking toward them from the gardens with his hands in his pockets. Caroline walked up to him.

"You did get the order to stop work here, didn't you?" she asked.

The man focused on her as if she were a species of animal he had never seen before.

"I what?" he asked.

"The order to stop working," she said. "We were at City Hall less than fifteen minutes ago. They're going to consider our petition to keep this park open."

"First I've heard of it, little lady," the bulldozer operator said. "My orders are to flatten this whole thing, and scoop out a big hole for the basement of a parking lot."

"But you got those orders before we saw the planning commission," Justine said.

"Little lady, if City Hall wanted me to stop, they'd have stopped me," the man said. "I have a supervisor who rides around from one site to the next. When I saw him he didn't say anything about stopping work."

"Would you please check with him again before you start?" Caroline begged. "I'm sure there's been some misunderstanding."

"I don't have to check with anyone," the man said, looking less patient now. "I have my job for the day, and if I'm behind on my schedule, I'm going to catch it from my supervisor. Now be good kids, go back to school, and leave me to do my work, will you?"

"But we're trying to save this park," Caroline said. "We gave them a petition."

"You're too late to save this park, honey," the man said. "Now, please, go back to school." He began to climb up onto his bulldozer. The big engine sprang to life with a growl.

Caroline looked around desperately. Many more kids from school had come to witness the confrontation.

A crazy idea was forming in Caroline's head. "We'll have to make a human wall," she shouted over the roar of the machinery. "We just have to stall him."

Alex turned to the other kids. "Stand in a line in front of the entrance," he said. "That guy will never mow us down. Quick, before he gets through!"

The response was mixed. "Are you joking?" someone yelled. "I'm not going to be squished under a bulldozer. What if he can't stop in time?" A few people moved into line with Caroline and her friends. Most of the others moved safely away, and a few hung back just far enough not to be mistaken for part of the wall.

"We have enough of us to block the entrance," Alex said. "Just stand firm."

Caroline reached across and slid her hand into Alex's. The bulldozer began to inch toward them. "Get out of the way, kids," the driver shouted. "I don't want anyone to get hurt."

"We're not moving," Caroline shouted back. "Please go check with your boss."

"I ain't checking," he called back. "I'm coming forward right now. If you guys aren't out of my way, you'll end up flatter than a pancake."

The bulldozer inched closer and closer. When it was just a couple of feet away from them, the man stopped and climbed down again.

"Now give me a break, kids," he begged, going up to them. "I have a job to do. If I don't do my job, I get in big trouble. I might even get fired. You don't want that, do you? I've got kids of my own. You don't want their old man to be out of work, do you? So please stand aside and let me do my job!"

"We're only asking you to go phone City Hall before you start," Caroline said. "That's not much to ask, is it?"

"I'm not allowed to leave my equipment," he said. "My boss would have come by right away if there were any change in plans. Now please go away, or I'll have to call the cops."

"I thought you weren't allowed to leave your equipment," Tracy told him.

"Okay. You asked for it," the man said. "Don't say I didn't warn you. This time I'm coming forward. If anyone is in my way, then too bad for them!"

As he finished this speech, the whole group was startled by a change in the pitch of the bulldozer's engine. They turned to see it backing away down the block.

"Hey, what the . . ." the driver yelled.

Caroline saw a petite figure at the bulldozer's controls, her blond hair streaming out behind her in the wind. "Chrissy!" Caroline screamed. "Chrissy, what are you doing?"

Chrissy didn't seem to have heard her. Her mouth was set in a grim line, and she frowned as she worked the controls. The bulldozer turned and began to move faster and faster down the hill.

"Come back!" the man yelled.

"Chrissy!" Caroline screamed again. She began to run after the bulldozer. The crowd ran behind her, yelling with delight. In front of her was the operator, purple with rage, and shaking his fist.

Caroline felt footsteps overtaking her. "Hold on, Chrissy, I'm coming!" Alex yelled. He ran easily past Caroline and sprinted after the disappearing bulldozer.

"Chrissy, what are you doing!" he yelled as he closed in behind her.

"I'm taking the bulldozer away so he can't mow anyone down," Chrissy yelled back.

"Chrissy, stop that thing right now!" Alex yelled back. "You'll kill yourself."

"I can't stop it yet. It's too close," she called back, not taking her eyes off the road.

Still running toward them, Caroline took in this whole scene with a strange mixture of fear and jealousy battling inside her. She certainly didn't want Chrissy hurt. But Alex seemed *awfully* worried. What Caroline saw next, however, erased every emotion except sheer panic from her mind. A black-and-white police car had screeched to a halt across the dozer's path a few feet ahead of it. Two uniformed cops with guns drawn jumped out. Chrissy brought the dozer to a stop.

"I think you'd better climb down and come with us, miss," one of them said.

As Caroline raced toward Chrissy, more police came streaming from the top of the hill. "All of you come quietly. There won't be any trouble if you just come quietly," a voice blared through a bullhorn. Even then Caroline didn't really take in the fact that the police were addressing her. She ran to the spot where two policemen were already bundling Chrissy into a police car.

"Wait, please, just a minute! I can explain!" Caroline yelled to them, but they didn't seem to hear her. Then she was grabbed and led in another direction.

Even though it wasn't really cold in her cell, Caroline could not stop shivering. Some of the other girls chatted and giggled nervously, but Caroline sat silently apart. The bulldozer driver had fingered her as the main troublemaker. What if the police let everyone else go and put her in prison as an example? Could a convict get into college? Where was Alex? Was he scared, too? And what about Chrissy? Why wasn't Chrissy here yet? Were they interrogating her under bright lights in a small room? *Poor Chrissy, I bet she's even more terrified than I am*, Caroline thought. *If she can't handle a big city high school, she must be miserable in the San Francisco jail.*

After what Caroline thought had been hours, the outer door clanged open and Chrissy was brought in. She saw Caroline immediately and rushed over to her with a big grin.

"Isn't this exciting?" she asked. "I bet you never thought something like this would happen to you."

"Are you kidding?" Caroline asked. "This has been the most horrible experience of my life. Weren't you even scared?" One look at Chrissy's face told Caroline it had been a waste of time to worry about her cousin.

Chrissy looked as if it had never occurred to her to be frightened. "They were very nice, considering I'm a criminal. They got me a soda while I was waiting, because it was hot in that room. The lady who's keeping our watches was really kind to me. She told me all sorts of stories about the good old days in San Francisco. Her daughter was a big protester in the sixties. I got the idea she's really all for what we're doing."

Caroline fought back her anger. Once again, Chrissy had created a mess, yet Caroline was the one who suffered. At least the current problem was big enough to keep her from plotting ways to get rid of Chrissy once and for all. "Do you think we'll have to stay in here all night?" Caroline asked flatly. "I don't really know what's happening anymore."

"They're phoning everyone's folks right now,"

Chrissy said, leaning back on the bench as if she were in an armchair at home. "When they put up bail for us, I guess we're free to go."

"I hope my parents are going to be understanding about this," Caroline said. At that thought, her mouth went so dry she could barely get the words out.

"Sure they will," Chrissy said. "You didn't do anything wrong. Just look at this as a good way of getting out of afternoon classes."

"Oh, no," Caroline gasped. "I completely forgot about school. We'll get in trouble for cutting classes on top of everything else."

"Don't you think jail might be a valid excuse?" Chrissy asked. She broke into a loud giggle. "If we have to stay all night, we won't be able to do our homework. I bet they never got jail as an excuse for not handing in homework before!"

"I don't know how you can find this funny, Chrissy," Caroline mumbled.

"Everything will work out fine. You'll see," Chrissy said. "This place is just like the sheriff's office in Danbury, only much bigger. We all used to pop in there on our way home from school when we were little kids. The sheriff was so nice. He kept this jar of jelly beans under the counter for us . . ."

I don't believe this, Caroline thought, staring at her cousin. *She is actually enjoying this. Will I ever learn? What next?*

Thirteen

"How could you do such a thing?" Caroline's mother demanded as the car swung out of the police lot toward home. "I thought you had seen last year the value of peaceful protest. And to get Chrissy involved in it! What am I going to tell your Aunt Ingrid? That I've had her daughter here for less than a month and already she's in jail?"

"It's not so bad, Mom," Caroline said. "I'm sure they'll understand in court." Not that she really believed it.

"They'll understand that Chrissy stole a bulldozer and drove off in it without a license," her father said grimly.

"But I had to do it, Uncle Richard," Chrissy said in a small voice from the backseat. "That man was about to drive over Caroline. The only way I could think of stopping him was to get his bulldozer out of the way."

"But you might have been killed!" Caroline's father said. "What on earth made you think you could drive a bulldozer? You told me you don't even know how to drive a car!"

"But I know how to drive farm machines," Chrissy said. "I drive a harvester sometimes, and all sorts of tractors. The driving was easy, but I got a little scared when it picked up speed going down the hill."

"Well, I just hope you don't both end up in juvenile hall and that your college chances aren't ruined forever," Caroline's mother said with a huge sigh. "And what is your principal going to say tomorrow?"

Caroline trembled at the thought. Mr. O'Brien wasn't the sort of principal who put up with dumb behavior.

She was trembling all over again the next morning as she approached his office with Chrissy and Alex. The attendance officer had sent them there the minute she laid eyes on their excuse notes for the day before.

"I saw you on the six o'clock news last night, Caroline," Dolores called as Caroline and Chrissy stalled outside Mr. O'Brien's office. "You looked good."

"Thanks," Caroline said weakly. She didn't feel at all good. Her stomach had turned into jelly sometime in the past twenty-four hours. She had not managed to eat a bite of supper the night before; at breakfast all she could manage was a swig of orange juice.

"What was it like, getting arrested?" one of the other girls wanted to know. Caroline was about to admit that it had been terrifying when Chrissy announced, "It was kind of fun. The people down at the police department were really nice to us." Dolores gave her that wide-eyed look once again, shook her head, and walked away.

"Do you really think he can suspend us, Alex?" Caroline whispered. "Will it go on our record and keep us out of college?"

Alex looked down at her with understanding. "We did what we thought was right, Cara. How can anyone blame us for that? We went to the right people, we asked them for time to reconsider, and they ignored us. I don't see how anyone could blame us for that."

"But we were disturbing the peace," Caroline said, her voice trembling with fright.

"You were disturbing the peace," Chrissy reminded her. "*I* was stealing a bulldozer. How crazy can you get? I tried to explain that I wasn't stealing it, I was just driving it. What would I want a bulldozer for? There's nowhere to keep it for starters."

Caroline looked at her and managed a weak grin. "It's okay for you," she said. "They can hardly suspend you in your first week of school. The very worst they can do is send you back to Iowa."

For a second Chrissy's face lit up, then she shook her head. "Nah, I wouldn't want to go home in disgrace. I'd never live it down. I'm glad my dad is a couple of thousand miles away, or he'd kill me for this. Just think of it. My cousin William is police chief over in Bloomfield. Your cousin too, Caroline."

Caroline was in no mood to find out that she had a cousin who was chief of police. "I suppose we'd better go in and get this over with," she said, turning her white face toward Alex.

"Hey, it's not the firing squad." He leaned down to brush her forehead with a kiss.

"It feels like it," she said, walking ahead to knock on the principal's door.

Mr. O'Brien scowled at them across his massive, polished wood desk.

"I understand that a group from this school, led by you three, left the campus yesterday without permission and tried to stop a city employee from doing his job. Is that correct?"

"Well, yes sir," Alex mumbled. "We had to leave the campus to take our petitions to City Hall, and—"

"Is it or is it not a school rule that students may not leave the campus without permission?" Mr. O'Brien asked coldly.

"Well, yes sir, it is, but we only intended to be off campus during lunch period, so—"

"So the school rule doesn't apply to lunch breaks?"

"Mr. O'Brien, it was very important for us to visit the planning commission as soon as possible," Caroline said. "We had to risk breaking a rule for something much more important. We did it for everyone's benefit. Everyone at school uses that park—"

Mr. O'Brien frowned. "What do you think it does for Maxwell's image when a group of you make the front page for getting yourselves arrested?" he demanded.

"I'm sorry, sir," Caroline mumbled. "We didn't mean to break any law. We couldn't think of anything else to do to stop the man with the bulldozer."

"You have to learn that you cannot take things into your own hands," Mr. O'Brien said dryly. "We have elected representatives to take our complaints to in government. You can't just start ignoring the law because you don't believe something is fair."

"But we had to act in a hurry, Mr. O'Brien," Alex said. "We found out that they were going to tear up our park, so we got signatures on a petition, and we took it to the planning commission."

"The commissioner we saw said she would present our petition to her board, Mr. O'Brien," Caroline interrupted. "But she knew that work was already due to start. She just lied to get us out of there! If we didn't act properly, then she didn't either!"

Mr. O'Brien's eyes narrowed. "That does not excuse your behavior up at the park," he said. "Harassing a city employee—"

"Harassing!" Chrissy burst out angrily. "He was harassing us! We were just standing there, and he started driving his bulldozer at us. Caroline kept trying to talk to him. She just asked him to phone his boss before he started, but he wouldn't listen. I had to take his 'dozer—"

The principal looked at her with interest. "So you were the one who stole the bulldozer?" he asked, and a smile flickered across his face.

"Yes, sir," Chrissy said meekly. "But I just borrowed it, really. I wanted to get it safely away from the crowd before that man squashed somebody flatter than a pancake like he threatened to!"

"He threatened to do that, did he?" Mr. O'Brien asked.

"Yes, sir," Chrissy said. "He used those very words."

"I see," he said. He looked down at his papers for a while without speaking.

"It appears," Mr. O'Brien said at last, "that circumstances provoked you to act the way you did. I'm not saying that I'm in favor of what you did, but you did try to act reasonably and peacefully, and I respect that. So I am going to drop this matter and I will write a letter to the magistrate when your case comes up in juvenile court next week. I also think you might find that the publicity you got last night will start a more orderly campaign to save the park. I just don't want you to think that you handled things in a reasonable, adult fashion." He closed the notebook on his desk with a thump that made them all jump. "Okay," he boomed. "Get out of here and get to your classes. And just don't let me catch you sneaking off campus again, or it will mean a suspension that will go on your records. Understand?"

"I can't believe it," Alex said as they came out into the hall. "He was actually on our side!"

"He's going to talk to the magistrate for us," Caroline squeaked. "It's going to be all right! Oh, Alex, I'm so relieved!"

"You're not the only one," Alex said, wrapping her into a tight hug.

A crowd began to gather in the hall. "What did the principal say?" "Is everything going to be okay?" "Did you get suspended?" they demanded.

"Are you the kid who stole the bulldozer?" a boy asked Chrissy.

"What? She stole a bulldozer? Are you kidding?"

"Yeah, man. Didn't you see her on the news last night? She drove it right out from under the old guy's nose. It was in this morning's paper!" Chrissy was suddenly the center of attention, her story buzzing through the crowd. A large group surrounded her.

"Way to go, Chrissy!" voices yelled as her drive down the hill was described again and again.

"Hey, there's our hero!" Marvin Jones announced loudly as he passed with his buddies. "That was the greatest thing I've seen since I've been at this school. Where'd you learn to drive like that?"

"Oh, I've driven much bigger things than that," Chrissy said with a grin. "You should see me behind the wheel of a harvester!"

"You've got to come to the football game on Friday night," Marvin told her. "We're playing Cardinal Newman, and they have a fullback they call the bulldozer. You two just gotta meet!"

Caroline stood silently in the crowd, watching Chrissy. She was lapping up every moment.

"How about that?" Chrissy asked Caroline as they walked home that afternoon. "Won't this be something to write my folks about? Only one week here, and already I've got my picture in the newspaper and everyone in the whole school knows who I am. And I've been invited to sit on the players' bench at the football game! And everybody is proud of me because the city said they'll hold up work on the park. I just can't get over it! This is the most exciting day of my life. I'm so glad I came here." And she danced like a little girl down the hill ahead of Caroline, who watched her with confusion. She ought to have been glad that Chrissy was so happy and a heroine at school, and especially that the park had been saved. But *she* had started the protest, she had formed the human wall to stop the bulldozer—and nobody seemed to care about those things anymore. And she wanted them to.

I'm being selfish and childish, Caroline told herself. *After all, it looks as if the park is going to be saved—what does it matter who gets the credit for it? I'm glad everything's gone so well for Chrissy, too. Now I won't have to be her baby-sitter all year.* That thought only made Caroline think about the crowd that had gathered around Chrissy in the hall that morning and she felt miserable all over again.

Late that evening Caroline sat in the window seat, trying to concentrate on a textbook. Chrissy had fallen into an easy slumber around ten as usual. She looked like a fragile china doll in the soft light of the room. Her long eyelashes touched her cheeks; her skin was as smooth as fine porcelain. Caroline was still too tense to sleep. How had this innocent-looking girl managed to turn her life upside down in a few short weeks?

I thought I knew who I was and where I was going before she arrived. Everything is different now. I've been trying to grow up and handle everything as a mature person would. Then along comes Chrissy, who acts totally naive and irresponsible and impetuous, yet everything seems to go just right for her! She takes chances and people admire her for it. Would I be happier if I'd never known I had a cousin Chrissy?

"Not in bed yet?" her mother asked gently, walking

up behind her and putting her hand on Caroline's shoulder.

"I was just thinking about going," Caroline said, not turning toward her mother. The way her parents had blamed her for Chrissy's behavior still hurt a lot.

"It's been a crazy two days, hasn't it?" her mother began awkwardly.

"You can say that again," Caroline answered, still looking down at the bay.

"I didn't think until later how very scared you must have been," her mother continued. "I'm sure the whole thing was difficult for you, sweetheart."

"It wasn't my favorite experience so far."

"Caroline?" her mother said in a soft voice. "About yesterday—I'm sorry. I came down on you pretty hard. You only did what you thought was right."

"You yelled at me for letting Chrissy do crazy things," Caroline said in a choked voice. "That wasn't fair. I'm not her nursemaid, you know. I was pretty busy worrying about a bulldozer running over me at the time!"

Her mother gave a little laugh. "I know, honey," she said. "And I want you to know that I think you were very brave. I overreacted yesterday. It's a shock for a parent to get a phone call and find out that her child has been arrested. All I could think was that this episode would start trouble all over again."

"What do you mean, Mom?" Caroline turned to face her mother for the first time.

"I mean that this sort of thing caused my original breakup with my family."

"I thought you said they didn't like Dad."

"Because he got arrested a couple of times, among other things."

"Dad? My dad? The one who always waits at crosswalks until the light turns green even when no traffic is coming? He got arrested?"

Her mother laughed. "We were both students in the sixties, Caroline. Students were a big part of the movement to stop the killing in Vietnam in those days. We did what you have just done. We protested peacefully. We actually thought we could make adults listen to us. Of course, they behaved just like the adults today—they arrested us. When my parents heard I'd been arrested, they hit the roof! From that moment on, they were prepared to dislike your father. My first reaction yesterday was that your aunt Ingrid would also hit the roof when she heard that her daughter had been arrested, and that she'd blame me. I don't ever want my family to break up again like that."

"I'm sure she'll understand, Mom," Caroline said. "And our principal is going to put in a good word for us, so I bet they'll drop the charges. Chrissy was pretty brave, you know. That man was going to drive that huge thing right at us."

Edith Kirby put her arm around her daughter's shoulder. "I think you were pretty brave, too. Very brave, in fact. Chrissy's the sort of person who likes making waves; you're not. When someone who is as naturally reserved and shy as you stands up to adults, it requires a lot of guts. I want you to know that I'm proud of you, Caroline."

"Thanks, Mom," Caroline said. She almost added that her mother seemed to be the only person who remembered that she had played any part at all, but she swallowed back the words.

"I guess I'd better be going to bed," she said.

"Would you like a hot drink first?"

"No thanks. I'll be fine."

"Good night, honey. Sleep well."

"Good night, Mom."

Fourteen

Caroline didn't go often to football games. She had never wanted to be a cheerleader or a member of the marching band or pep squad, and she usually went to games when school spirit demanded that everyone be present—on homecoming night and when Maxwell played its biggest rivals. But as soon as the girls arrived at the field, it was clear that football had been an important part of Chrissy's life.

"Oh, does this ever make me homesick," she said. "When I see those cheerleaders out there, I realize that would be me back at home. This is the first year I haven't been a cheerleader since seventh grade."

"Maybe you could try out for the Maxwell squad," Caroline suggested.

Chrissy shook her head. "It wouldn't be the same, she said. "The routines are really different and I still don't feel like Maxwell is my school. And I've always had Ben to cheer for—that made it special. Besides," she added, counting across the field. "You only have twelve cheerleaders!"

"That's what most schools have around here," Caroline said. "Do you have more?"

"I'll say," Chrissy said. "We have three hundred students. Out of those, I'd reckon eighty percent of the boys are on football teams and eighty percent of the girls are cheerleaders or pom-pom girls. It's the big thing. Every little boy grows up wanting to play football, and every little girl wants to be a cheerleader. That's just the way it is." Her face took on a wistful look. "In Danbury, a thief could break into any house he liked on a Friday night because every family would be at the football game. There's even a big traffic jam Friday nights—and that's something you don't see much of where I live. Every car has a 'GO HORNETS' bumper sticker and even parents wear black and gold on game days."

Caroline stopped herself from saying that there probably wasn't much else to do on Friday nights in Danbury. Instead she listened politely while Chrissy described all the district championships the Hornets had won, how they made it to the state tournament in nineteen eighty-two, and how most senior players went to college on football scholarships. Chrissy knew all the names and numbers.

At school that day, Marvin had invited Chrissy and Caroline to sit on the players' bench. Caroline was conscious of being in full view of everyone in the stands, and even more self-conscious after the game began and

Chrissy began cheering. She showed how well she knew the game, yelling out praise or criticism after every play.

"Hey, what about your tight end?" she'd yell, her high voice carrying over the roar of the crowd and the deep growl of the coach. "He's wide open, and you keep waiting for your wide receiver . . ." Then she'd sit down again in disgust. "Phew," she commented at the end of the first quarter. "You guys sure don't know too much about football."

Caroline couldn't stop herself this time. "Well, Maxwell is pretty much an academic high school. It's not really cool to take football so seriously."

But during the second quarter, as it became clear that Chrissy knew what she was talking about, several players wandered over to talk to her when they weren't on the field. They squatted beside Chrissy and Caroline, like ocean liners moored beside a couple of tugboats, and argued each play with Chrissy, laughing with her when the results on the field proved her right.

At half time, Chrissy was to be called onto the field to meet Cardinal Newman's Bulldozer. Chrissy was taken away by the pep squad at the beginning of the half-time show, and the players all had disappeared into the locker room, leaving Caroline to feel alone and stupid on her bench. The band played, the majorettes twirled, and the pom-pom girls did their dance routine, but Caroline saw no sign of Chrissy. Then the field cleared, and the Newman team came out to warm up for the second half. Then the loudspeaker blared, "Too bad about the Bulldozer, Cardinal Newman, because we just got ourselves a Bulldozer tamer!"

Just as the players dropped to the field for push-ups, an old yellow convertible—thinly disguised as a bulldozer—chugged onto the field. Chrissy and Marvin sat atop the backseat.

"Here she is, folks," the announcer shouted. "The little lady who fought City Hall and won, Chrissy Madden, all the way from Iowa! We say welcome to California, Chrissy, and thanks from Maxwell High!"

Chrissy drove around the field once to cheers, then stopped to shake hands with the Bulldozer from the other team. Caroline thought she was going to be sick.

At Justine's victory party later that evening, Caroline sat apart from the others at the edge of Justine's deck, watching the fog move in to swallow up the lights across the bay. Justine had decided to throw a party for a few friends, but those friends had invited their friends, so Justine's deck creaked under the weight of half the students of Maxwell High. Caroline felt claustrophobic in the crowd, so right after she had finished her barbequed ribs, she had wandered off to sit alone and try to straighten out her thoughts.

Everyone else is so happy tonight, she thought. *I should be happy, too, I guess. I should be glad that so many good things have been happening to Chrissy.* She paused and reflected. *Maybe I think too many good things have been happening to her. She's been handed life in California on a plate, and I worked so hard to be liked and accepted. Everyone thinks she's the greatest thing since pizza.*

Caroline shifted uncomfortably in her seat and thought of how her stomach had dropped at the sound of all the applause for Maxwell's Bulldozer tamer. No one seemed to remember who had organized the campaign to stop the bulldozer in the first place. Caroline couldn't deny it; she was jealous of all the attention Chrissy had been getting.

A cold wind swept across the deck, making Caroline shiver. She pulled her jacket tighter around her and turned up its collar. On the other side of the deck, someone was singing along with a guitar, a haunting song in a minor key; Caroline couldn't catch the words. Farther away still, people suddenly burst into laughter at someone's joke.

A tap on the shoulder startled Caroline.

"Oh, there you are. I've been looking for you," Alex said, sliding into the space beside her. "Why are you hiding?"

"I'm not hiding," Caroline said. "I just felt like getting away. It got too noisy when everyone started singing."

"They're a little carried away, I guess," Alex said. "They're singing ancient protest songs to celebrate our being here tonight and not in jail. This has been the craziest week, hasn't it?"

"Uh-huh," Caroline agreed.

"I guess more than one good thing came out of it for you," Alex said.

"What do you mean?"

"Well," said Alex, "not only have you possibly saved a park from destruction, but you've had a chance to see that your country cousin will obviously have no problem making it in the big city." He smiled broadly. "Remember when you came up to my house before she got here? You were so worried that she wouldn't fit in.

You thought that none of your friends would like her and that she'd be clinging to you all year. Now look at her—she's everyone's big hero, isn't she?"

"I guess she is."

"And wasn't she terrific at the football game?"

"Yeah, terrific."

Alex took Caroline's hand. "Come on back to the party," he said. "You're freezing to death over here near the water."

Caroline allowed herself to be led back toward the crowd. Loud cheers and laughter were coming from a picnic table where Chrissy was sitting across from one of the guys from the football team.

"They're having an arm-wrestling contest," Tracy whispered as Caroline squeezed into the circle with Alex. "Chrissy already beat Todd. You should have seen his face. That girl is strong. Don't get on the wrong side of her, Caroline, or you'll be in big trouble."

"I'll remember that," Caroline said flatly.

The boy finally forced Chrissy's arm down amid cheers and hisses. "Great match, Sean," someone jeered. "Look how much you weigh compared to her. I bet she's not more than a hundred pounds. You must be at least one eighty!"

Sean blushed beet red. "She's pretty strong," he protested. "I had to use all my weight to beat her."

"Find a guy who's more her size," someone else called. Tracy grabbed Alex. "Go on, Alex. You're not a big, overweight ox," she said, laughing as she pushed him forward.

Alex slid into the seat across from Chrissy. Chrissy grinned shyly at him as he locked his hand in hers. "One, two, three . . . go!" Tracy called. Staring fiercely into each other's eyes, they struggled silently, motionlessly, their hands gripped tightly, their arms brushing for an eternity. Caroline couldn't see Alex's eyes from where she was standing, but Chrissy's were very bright.

Just when Caroline thought she couldn't stand it for a moment longer, just when she wanted to rush in and break them apart, Chrissy's hand began to sink slowly. Her eyes didn't leave Alex's face for a second until her arm was on the table, and Alex got up amid cheers.

"They're right, that girl is strong," he commented as he came back to Caroline. "I wouldn't like to be a hog who got away from her." He laughed lightly, but Caroline sensed uneasiness in his voice. *What had he felt when Chrissy gazed into his eyes? Was that shine in Chrissy's eyes coming from the excitement of the competition, or was it reflecting something she had seen in Alex's eyes?* Caroline recalled the look of concern in Alex's eyes as he had raced after the bulldozer the other day. "She's everyone's big hero," he had said. Did he include himself in her list of fans, or was he beginning to admire her even more than the others?

Caroline pushed her way out of the circle again and stood alone, watching the fading red of the dying barbeque embers. Her stomach was clenching itself into a tight knot of fear. She was pretty sure that Chrissy had let Alex win. Why? She was clearly enjoying beating the other boys. She wouldn't really make a play for

Alex, would she? She still talked all the time about her boyfriend at home. She wrote him letters and played the tape he sent her over and over. But Ben was far, far away and Alex, Caroline knew, was a really cute guy. Was Chrissy planning to take over that part of her life, too?

Fifteen

Caroline walked slowly up the hill toward home. Every muscle in her body ached, and today the slope seemed to have grown to the size of Mt. Everest, stretching up and up without end. Her ballet bag felt as if it were filled with lead instead of ballet slippers, a leotard, and a towel.

I'd love to fall asleep right now, she thought, *but I have that French essay waiting for me at home.* She frowned. *I wonder if Chrissy's there.*

It would be so much easier to collapse in her room if she didn't have to worry about someone else bursting in, yelling the way Chrissy always yelled, slamming doors the way Chrissy always slammed them. Chrissy hadn't done anything wrong in particular in the past couple of weeks, but nearly everything she did seemed to annoy Caroline. *Maybe I'm just tense about the per-*

formance and looking for someone to take it out on, Caroline thought. It would be the first time she had danced on a big stage, in front of an audience who had paid for tickets to the performance. It was even rumored around school that the head of the San Francisco Ballet came to watch these performances and scout for future students.

Hardly me, the way I've been dancing, Caroline decided with a sigh. Her ballet teacher had made that very clear about an hour earlier.

"You're not concentrating, Caroline," she had yelled in front of the whole class. "Look at your line! You're spoiling the entire effect." After class she had taken Caroline aside. "I thought you were ready for this," she had said in her clipped voice. "Now I'm not so sure. There are too many errors, Caroline. You've got to put your heart into it. No more goofing off, as you say. Remember, I have plenty of pupils who would give anything to take your place in this company."

Caroline shivered as she went over those words in her mind, even though the evening was not cold. *What would my parents say if I was kicked out of the company?* she wondered. *What would I tell the kids at school? They've already told me they're all coming to the performance. Madame thinks I'm goofing off! If that weren't so tragic, it would almost be funny, because nobody could have been working harder than I've been. Every teacher in the world wants one hundred percent of your time and thinks you're goofing off if you give some of that time to other subjects.*

"It's child abuse, that's what it is," Caroline muttered as she dragged her feet up the flight of steep steps to the front door. "All I want is ten minutes of peace . . ."

"Caroline, you've just got to help me," Chrissy yelled, her voice echoing down the hall the moment Caroline closed the front door.

"What is it, Chrissy?" Caroline asked, making no effort to hide the impatience in her voice.

Chrissy looked up from her paper-strewn bed and waved a mimeographed page in Caroline's direction. "It's algebra. I have this assignment due tomorrow, and I don't understand any of it. We never did stuff like this at home. How can an equation full of numbers make a curve? It doesn't make any sense to me, and I've got to get it done before I go out tonight."

"You're going out?" Caroline asked.

"Yeah, another movie," Chrissy said.

"Chrissy, you've seen three movies this week!" Caroline said. "Your allowance for the year is going to be used up by October at this rate!"

Chrissy gave a weak grin. "I know," she said. "But it's still so exciting for me. They only change the movie once a month in Danbury, and it's usually so old it's *Snow White* or *Bambi* or something. I've actually seen three brand new movies this week. I can't wait to write home about it—the boys will be green all over!"

She beamed at Caroline, her face lit with excitement so that Caroline felt like an old grouch being mad at her. She opened her mouth to say that algebra would never get easier if Chrissy rushed to go out every night, but she swallowed hard and managed to smile instead.

"I'm glad you're having a good time here," she said. "Remember when you thought you'd never fit in?"

A big grin spread over Chrissy's face. "I've made such good friends here, thanks to you," she said. "Everyone is so nice to me."

"That's great, Chrissy," Caroline said halfheartedly, flopping down onto her own neat bed.

"Is something wrong?" Chrissy asked, looking down with concern at her cousin.

Caroline sighed. "No, nothing's wrong," she said. "I'm just beginning to feel the pressure of junior year, I guess. I have a long French essay to do, and I don't know any of the vocabulary, and my ballet teacher has been bugging me for not practicing enough, and she's threatening to kick me out of the performing ensemble. There just aren't enough hours in a day any more."

Chrissy let the arm holding the paper fall to her side. "Gee, I'm sorry," she said. "Then I won't bug you about the algebra. I'll get it figured out somehow. Maybe Tracy can help me with it—or George. He's a math whiz, isn't he?"

Caroline nodded. "There's spaghetti in the fridge we can warm up for dinner," she said. "My folks won't be home until late from the concert."

"Oh, don't bother about dinner for me," Chrissy said brightly. "We'll all go out for pizza after the movie."

She jumped up from the bed, scattering papers in all directions, and began rummaging through her closet.

"Why is nothing I've got right to wear?" she asked with a sigh. "It's either way too hot or way too cold. I don't have any in-between clothes at all. I can't wear these old jeans again to the movies, can I?"

"Sure you can. You look fine," Caroline said wearily.

"Are you sure?" Chrissy asked. "You're not just saying that? I don't want to be the worst-dressed person there. These really need something to contrast with them—a nice bright color—and my clothes are all so blah."

"You can borrow my new turquoise jacket if you want," Caroline said.

"Really, truly?" Chrissy asked. "You are so nice. I know—I'll wear it with my black pants. I'll be extra careful, I promise."

She slipped her arms into the jacket and stood looking at herself in the mirror. "Ben was right," she said with a sigh. "He said I'd turn into a sophisticated city girl, and here I am. Look at me. I hardly recognize myself anymore. Justine thinks I should get my hair cut real short. Maybe I will. Make way, world, for the new, improved Chrissy Madden, with added brighteners!"

She spun around and knocked into her bed, sending more papers fluttering to the floor. "Whoops," she said, stooping to pick them up. "I guess I'd better get out of here. Bye, Cara. Thanks for the jacket. I'll bring you back a slice of pizza if you want!"

"That's okay," Caroline said. "I'll be asleep by the time you get back. Have fun."

"I sure will," Chrissy said. She bounded out of the room. Caroline heard her footsteps down the hall followed by the hard slam of the front door. She thought about dinner, then about her French essay. "I'd better start working," she announced to the empty room. She sat down at her desk. A half hour later, she still was staring at an empty page, her pen gripped tightly between her fingers. Words from her French dictionary swam in front of her eyes.

"What's the matter with me?" she asked out loud. "Why can't I seem to concentrate anymore? Is it just that I'm trying to do too much?"

She began to draw doodles in the margin of her paper. Every doodle suggested tall, lanky girls leaping around the page. *Is it really Chrissy?* she thought. *Is my problem really that Chrissy bugs me? I know she doesn't mean to, yet everything she does seems to be designed to spite me.*

You wanted her to settle in well, she reminded herself. *You were afraid she wouldn't fit in with your friends. Well, now she's settled in. You should be happy.*

But I didn't want her to settle in so well, Caroline thought miserably. *I didn't want* my *friends to become her friends. I didn't want* my *group to forget all about me.*

Ever since the incident with the bulldozer, Chrissy had become a celebrity around school. Now it seemed that there was nobody at Maxwell who didn't know her.

"Hey, Chrissy!" boys would yell out to her as they passed in the halls. "Show us your bulldozer muscles!"

And Chrissy would not blush or pretend she hadn't heard, as Caroline would have done. She would turn around and yell right back, "I never show my muscles in public!"

None of Caroline's friends yelled things after boys or talked back when strangers flirted with them. Caroline had always believed that kind of behavior was tacky, and she assumed her friends thought so, too. But nobody seemed to think Chrissy was being tacky except her. They all called Chrissy a good sport, and they liked her. *Better than me?* Caroline wondered. *Is that why I'm so annoyed with her, because I'm jealous that she gets along with people better than I do?*

It wasn't the first time Caroline had had to confront the possibility that she was jealous of Chrissy. And it all went back to the issue of who had gotten credit for saving the park, something that had already faded from most people's minds, except for Chrissy's new nickname. *It's just not fair,* Caroline thought, furiously drawing more doodles—this time of trees and bushes. *I was the one who got the petition going. I was the one who spoke up at City Hall. I was even the one who decided to form the human wall. But everyone has forgotten those things.*

What does that matter? Caroline asked herself. *Now you really are being petty. We saved the park, didn't we? The publicity made them stop construction. I know in my heart that I played a big part in helping to save it, so I can be proud of myself. It shouldn't matter to me what anyone else believes.*

But it did matter. Caroline admitted it to herself. A part of her had always dreamed of being popular and respected at school. When she had helped save the historic houses the year before and had been interviewed by the paper, she felt the glow of pride that people at school finally knew her name. Now she was just a nobody people passed in the halls again.

But it was even worse than that, this time. Caroline's

own friends seemed to have adopted Chrissy into their group, and it didn't seem to matter to anyone whether Caroline was a part of it or not, anymore. Chrissy had taken her place.

Was Alex with them? Caroline wondered, feeling a sudden stab of jealousy so strong that it almost physically hurt. Neither Alex nor Chrissy had given her any concrete reason to be suspicious or jealous since the night of Justine's party when the notion had first occurred to Caroline. Since then, Caroline had tried to put the idea out of her mind. Chrissy hadn't even mentioned that Alex was going to the movie, but he couldn't be expected to stay home just because his girl friend had two hours of dance class and French homework. The thought of the French essay forced Caroline's attention back to the doodle-covered paper. She crumpled it into a ball, threw it away, and pulled out a fresh sheet. "The principal ports on the Mediterranean Sea," she began—but she had to stop and look up the word for port. At this rate, it was going to take her all night to describe all the geographical features of France.

A picture of Alex flashed into her mind, unbidden, Alex standing on the deck of his father's sailboat, his hair blowing in the wind. Alex had not yet complained again about the small amount of time she could give him, but how much neglect would a guy put up with? Or if Chrissy was around all the time, would he have to put up with neglect at all? Perhaps Chrissy felt obligated to Alex for the way he had tried to save her from the bulldozer. It was a dumb, crazy thing to have done. He could have been seriously hurt, yet he had risked it for Chrissy. He had also been the one to pull Chrissy from the ocean. Did it all mean something? Or was Alex just a wonderful guy who would have done the same for anyone? She could find out if Alex and Chrissy were together simply by calling. But what if she found out they were together? Maybe it was better not to know.

"Stop this nonsense," Caroline scolded herself. "Chrissy went to a movie with a group of your friends. That's all. Now quit worrying and start describing the port of Marseilles."

She gazed across the room for inspiration, but her eyes met only the pile of clothes, lying, as always, on Chrissy's side of the floor.

Even sharing the room had become hard for Caroline to bear. She had always kept her room just the way she wanted it. Her favorite posters had lined the walls, and her favorite stuffed animals gazed neatly and cheerfully up at her from the foot of her bed. It had been a friendly, welcoming room, the sort of place you could escape to after a bad day, the sort of place where you could lie on your bed and daydream for hours if you wanted to. But now it was Chrissy's room, too. Chrissy's half was always messy, and Chrissy was always bursting in and out without warning.

I really miss my privacy, Caroline thought miserably. *I never seem to have a minute to myself anymore.* Then she had to laugh in spite of herself. *Caroline Kirby, a minute ago you were complaining because Chrissy went out with your friends and left you all alone.*

Caroline took up her pencil, chewed on the end, and began to write again. After a half hour, she had one page finished, and her concentration wavered again. She got up and wandered into the kitchen, looked at the spaghetti lying cold and appetizing in its pot, grabbed a peach, and left the kitchen. Suddenly the house seemed too quiet. She could hear the street noises coming up from outside—the clanging of the cable-car bell as it made the turn down to the bay, a distant fog horn from the Golden Gate, the revving of a sports car engine as it climbed the hill. So much was happening, and she wasn't part of any of it.

I will phone Alex, she thought. *I have no reason except my own insecurity to think he's falling for Chrissy. We haven't had a long talk in days. I really miss him.*

The phone rang several times before it was picked up.

"Caroline?" Alex's mother's voice came crisp and clear across the line. "Alex isn't home, honey. He went out about an hour ago. I think he said he was going to a movie. Did you want him to call you back when he gets in?"

"No thanks, I'll see him in the morning," Caroline said as she hung up.

She walked back to her room again, the peach half-eaten in her hand. Alex had gone to the movie without her. She sat down, staring out of the window, trying not to cry about something so trivial, yet feeling herself swamped with loneliness. She was still sitting, staring, a trickle of tears stinging her cheeks, when the doorbell rang.

"Oh, rats," she muttered, pushing herself away from her desk. "And Mom and Dad aren't even home." Her parents' friends had the habit of dropping in unexpectedly, and the thought of having to be polite and entertain them was too much tonight. She opened the door slowly.

"Who were you expecting, the Boston Strangler?" Alex asked with a grin.

"Oh, Alex, it's you!" she exclaimed delightedly.

"Is it so amazing that I should come and visit my girl friend sometimes?" he asked, putting his hands onto her shoulders and drawing her toward him.

"I thought you'd gone to a movie with the rest of them," Caroline said.

"Boring movie," Alex answered, planting a little kiss on her forehead, then steering her into the house, his arm firmly around her shoulder. "I stayed exactly fifteen minutes. Long enough for the evil emperor to have thrown five people into a boiling pit and fed two to his pet monsters. Then I decided I had to come over and see you, even if you were busy and were going to throw me out after five minutes."

Caroline wrapped her arms around his neck. "Oh, Alex," she said. "I am so glad you came. I'd been feeling so down . . ."

He brought his lips towards hers in a gentle kiss. "Does that make you feel better?" he asked.

"A little," she said, her eyes teasing him.

He kissed her again. This time his lips were warm and demanding. The kiss lasted a long time. When they broke apart, Caroline was slightly breathless.

"Now are you feeling better?" he asked.

"Much," she said, "And you'd better not kiss me like that again, or I'll forget all about the French essay on my desk that is only half-written."

"You want some help?" he asked. "I've already done mine. I know the words for mountains and valleys and agriculture and all kinds of impressive things."

"I'd love some help," she said. "In fact I'd like you to write it for me, but I don't really want to cheat. Come and sit next to me and feed me words like a walking dictionary."

She took his hand, and they walked to her room.

"Where is everybody?" Alex asked.

"Mom and Dad had to go to a concert—some new singer who sounds as if she's gargling."

Alex's eyes lit up. "So I'm all alone in the apartment with you?"

"With me and my French essay," she said. "In case you get any strange ideas."

"You forget you're talking to a former Boy Scout," Alex said, sitting down on her bed and smiling up at her. "So why were you feeling down tonight? Because you couldn't go to the movie? You didn't miss a thing!"

Caroline managed a weak smile. "I guess I was feeling sore at Chrissy," she said.

"Chrissy—what on earth has she done? She's always so sweet."

Caroline winced. "Exactly. She is so sweet and everyone likes her and my parents think she's the greatest and so does everyone in the school and she gets to go everywhere."

"Do I detect a note of jealousy here?" Alex asked innocently.

"Of course not," Caroline said. "I'm not jealous of Chrissy, and I do want her to have a good time here, and she is very nice. It's just that everything in life seems to be going so smoothly for her when everything's so hard for me."

"What are you talking about?" Alex asked. "You're doing great at everything! You've made the honor society at school. You've been chosen for the performing company at your ballet school. You have me for a boyfriend. What more could you want from life?"

Caroline had to laugh. "When you put it like that, it does sound good," she said. "But it's just that I have to work so hard to achieve those things. I have to do hours of homework every night and hours of ballet practice—"

"And hours of keeping me happy," Alex quipped.

Caroline reached over and threw her quilted cat pillow at him.

"Be serious for a minute," she said. "I'm ready to snap, Alex. I feel like I never have a moment for myself anymore. Everywhere I go, Chrissy is there. I can't even get to my bathroom when I want it. I don't even have my own room to myself."

Alex looked at her steadily, his brown eyes serious now. "What you are going through is called sibling rivalry," he said. "It's what goes on all the time in households with more than one child—all the fights for the bathroom and fights for territory in the bedroom and fights for a peaceful corner to do homework and fights for parents' attention. We kids with brothers and sisters have had to go through it all our lives. We've grown up racing each other to the bathroom door and pushing each other off our parents' laps. You've just found yourself with an instant sibling, and it's going to take you awhile to adjust."

"I guess so," Caroline said. "It's just so hard, Alex. Everything is so hard for me. I hate having someone bursting into my room without knocking and talking to me while I'm trying to do homework, and I hate having someone to compete with at school. Right when I was beginning to feel good about myself, someone comes along who everyone likes better . . ."

"Hey, that's not true and you know it," Alex said firmly. "Everyone is nice to Chrissy because she is new here and because she is a likeable person. If they take her out in the evenings, it doesn't mean they have forgotten you."

"It seems like that to me," Caroline said.

"So would you want the rest of us to stay home if you couldn't go out?" Alex asked.

"Of course not," Caroline said.

"And would you want Chrissy to stay home if you couldn't go with her?"

"No."

"Then what's the problem?" Alex asked. "We'd rather have you there with us, but we're not asking Chrissy as a substitute. She's not taking your place. She's become another friend. That's all."

"Sometimes . . ." Caroline began. "Sometimes I wonder how good a friend she's becoming."

"What do you mean?" Alex said. "Everyone likes her a lot."

"I'm not worried about everyone, Alex. I wonder how good a friend of yours she's becoming. You were the one who saved her when she took off on that bulldozer, and you were the one who was there first when she got knocked over at the beach."

Alex frowned. "Come on, Caroline. Don't look for trouble where there is none. Chrissy, who happens to be the cousin of the girl I care about, needed help, so I tried to help her. That's all there was to it. Now why don't you forget all that and let me show you how much I do care about you?" He leaned toward Caroline for a kiss, but she stopped him by placing both hands on his chest and pushing him away.

"So you don't find Chrissy attractive?"

"Of course, she's attractive. She's a tall, blond, pretty girl. But she's not the girl for me."

But Alex still hadn't said what Caroline wanted to hear. She needed for him to tell her directly that he would never get involved with Chrissy.

"Alex, suppose Chrissy made a play for you. Can you honestly tell me you would not be interested under any circumstances?"

She felt Alex's arm stiffen around her and saw his expression go hard. She knew instantly that she had gone too far. "What is with you, Cara?" he asked, his voice tight. "It's bad enough that I don't ever get to see you anymore. But it's really a drag when I take off from a movie just to come be with you, and instead of being happy to see me you practically accuse me of fooling around with your cousin. I told you I wasn't interested in her."

Fear tightened Caroline's stomach. Alex was right. She was acting foolish, exposing insecurities she should have resolved on her own. Caroline reached up to touch Alex's face. "I know, Alex. You're right. I'm sorry. It's just hard for me to get used to having her around. Will you forgive me?"

But instead of taking her in his arms as Caroline hoped he would, Alex reached up and removed Caroline's hand from his cheek. "Listen, Caroline. I think I'd better go now. Suddenly I'm not in a very good mood. Sorry. I'll talk to you later." He bent over and kissed Caroline quickly on the forehead, then strode toward the front door, his jaw tense with anger.

At the sound of the door shutting behind him, Caroline dropped to the sofa. Why had she pushed so far? What had made her drive Alex away like that? Was she going to let Chrissy Madden ruin her whole life before the year was over? The tears that had disappeared when Alex arrived sprang to her eyes again. Caroline sat and felt them trickle slowly down her cheek for a long time before she got up and returned to her room to face her French homework again.

Sixteen

For the next few weeks, ballet kept Caroline's mind off her problems with Alex, Chrissy, and school. Rehearsals were now every evening, and she hardly had a moment to see her friends or even talk with her parents. Some nights the rehearsals went well, and Caroline floated home on a cloud of anticipation, the music still pounding in her head as she played over and over the exquisite feeling of knowing she had moved in complete harmony with eleven other people, one limb of one giant, graceful, beautiful creature.

Other nights, the rehearsals did not go so smoothly. Madame yelled and even threw things in frustration. Caroline hated any conflict, so even if Madame's anger was not directed at her, she came home emotionally exhausted. At least as Madame yelled and taunted them, the dancers began to feel that they were all fellow sufferers under one tyrant, so that they were united by their sympathy for one another rather than competing for a place in the spotlight. Caroline suspected that it was part of Madame's plan to drive them all closer together; she obviously knew that after every session of her yelling and stomping, the troupe danced so much better and held their line so much more perfectly.

As rehearsals drew to a close, no one was quite so terrified by Madame anymore. One night Madame had been eating a banana and suddenly had thrown it down in disgust in front of Caroline. "Arms! Arms! What are the arms supposed to be doing?" she had screamed. Caroline had been in the middle of a forward leap and had landed on the banana, squashing it flat on the floor. She really hadn't intended to step on it, but she hadn't been able to change direction. The other dancers, however, thought that she had deliberately squashed Madame's banana and looked at it as a wonderful act of defiance. They had all burst out laughing when it happened; afterward in the changing room they had clustered around Caroline to tell her that she was a heroine.

On that night, Caroline came home excited and longing to wear the lilac tutu and dance for the world. On other nights, things did not go so well. Her body felt as if it were made of lead, her leaps seemed only to clear the ground by inches, and she could not lift one foot above her head without its wobbling. She even lost her balance one evening and bumped into the girl next to her.

"Watch out," the girl hissed. "You nearly knocked me over. You're on the wrong foot."

Caroline expected Madame to yell at any moment, and she slunk away gratefully as soon as rehearsal ended. She went over the steps in her head all the way home, angry at making a fool of herself in front of the others.

The pace of rehearsals had left Caroline with no time to concentrate on solving her problem with Alex, but she couldn't deny that she did have a problem with him. Since the night of their argument, he hadn't brought it up again, but Caroline had noticed a change in him. She had been too ashamed to bring it up herself or to apologize. Besides, the only time she ever got to see Alex was in the middle of a crowd; the rest of her time was spent dancing or keeping up with homework. But he had definitely been acting differently; he had become distant, almost secretive. Caroline could only hope that he would stick with her until after her performance was over; then she would have a chance to make it all up to him. She found out how foolish that hope was the day before the show.

On that day, with just ten minutes left to lunch period, Caroline was hurrying down the hall, giving a quick glance at the clock on the wall.

Great, she thought. *Now I've barely got time to eat. Why do I have to be a good student? Why couldn't I have been born a flaky kid who didn't care about grades or pleasing my parents or the future?*

The rest of her lunch hour had just been swallowed up in a discussion with her English teacher. He had called her up after class to say how much he enjoyed her latest essay and that he was planning to recommend her for honors English in the next semester. The conversation turned to the sort of books she would be expected to read for honors class, and then spread to a general discussion of Mr. Henshaw's opinions of literature. Caroline knew from the growling of her stomach that lunch hour was flying by, but she didn't want to stop Mr. Henshaw.

So she stayed, dutiful look of interest pasted on her face, until Mr. Henshaw himself had noticed the time. "Heavens above, it's almost one," he had said. "You poor child. You won't get a thing to eat if you don't hurry. You should have warned me I was talking too long. I know I ramble on and on once I get started. I've enjoyed our talk, Caroline. You'll do well in honors English."

Caroline finally reached her locker, wrenched it open, and took out her lunch bag. *No point in trying to make it to the park today,* she thought. *I'll just go sit in the sun in a quiet corner for ten minutes and get my head together before chemistry.*

She found a sheltered spot in the courtyard, leaned her back against the warm brick of the wall and halfheartedly ate her sandwich. Lately even her appetite hadn't been too great. *If only I could stop worrying about so many things,* she thought, putting the half-finished turkey sandwich back into its bag and trying the apple instead. *If only life weren't crammed so full of good grades and dance performances and cousins to compete with.*

Of course, it was harder than ever even to think about Chrissy. Between Caroline's rehearsals and Chrissy's busy social life, Caroline had managed to avoid all but the most necessary conversation with her cousin. Even if Chrissy wasn't actually fooling around with Alex, her very existence had driven an immoveable wedge between Caroline and him. Alex, fortunately, hadn't mentioned Caroline's suspicions to Chrissy or anyone else. At least, no one had said anything to Caroline, thank goodness. The thought of all her friends laughing at her silly jealousy behind her back would have been more than she could bear.

Caroline finished her apple, collected her books, and started to walk in from the courtyard. A carefree laugh floated out through an open window as she passed. *That sounds like Chrissy,* she thought.

She glanced inside. Then she froze like a statue, hiding in the deep shadow outside the window. Chrissy was standing with Alex in the hallway. They were leaning close together; Alex's hand was resting on the wall inches from Chrissy's face. It was such an intimate pose—the pose of two people in private conversation—that Caroline felt as if she'd been slapped in the face. She wanted to hurry away, but she couldn't make her feet leave the spot. She knew she didn't want to listen in on their conversation, to find out all her horrible suspicions were true after all, but she couldn't help herself.

But they were talking in low voices, and Caroline couldn't hear anything that made sense until she heard Alex say, "And she still doesn't suspect anything?"

"Not a thing," Chrissy said and laughed again. This time it didn't sound like a carefree, innocent laugh. It was the sort of laugh that you might expect from evil women on soap operas. The whole scene was like something from a bad soap opera.

Alex slid his hand over until it rested on Chrissy's shoulder. "Chrissy, this is going to be great," he said. "I can hardly wait."

"Me either," Chrissy whispered. She beamed up at him adoringly.

Caroline stifled the sob that almost came to her throat. She hurried down the courtyard to an entrance at the far end. "What a total dummy I was! To think that I ever worried about how my poor, hick cousin would fit into my sophisticated world!"

"Hey, Caroline, wait up!" Caroline jumped as if she had received an electric shock as a hand grabbed at her arm. She focussed on Maria, standing in the hall beside her, grinning as if this were the most normal day in the world.

"What's the big hurry?" Maria asked. "Are you in training for the marathon? You were sprinting down the hall like you were late for class, and there's five minutes of lunch left."

"Oh, okay," Caroline mumbled.

Maria eyed her quizzically. "Cara, is something wrong? You look as if you've seen a ghost."

"Wrong? No, nothing's wrong. Everything's just fine," Caroline said, turning away from Maria.

"Cara—look, something is wrong, I can tell. You want to talk about it? Maybe I can help."

Caroline hesitated. She had never been the type of person who blabbed about her troubles. It was hard for her to talk about things that affected her deeply.

"I don't think you can help, Maria," she said softly.

"Try me," Maria said, not willing to give up. "After all, we are friends, aren't we? You know what I'm like when I have problems. I cry all over everyone's shoulders. I know you're not like that, but it does help sometimes to talk about something that's getting to you."

"I don't think anyone can help this time," Caroline said bleakly. "I have to sort it out for myself. I have to decide what I want to do about it."

"About what?" Maria demanded.

"Chrissy and Alex," Caroline said.

"What about them?" Maria sounded surprised.

"You don't have to pretend nothing's going on," Caroline said. "I saw them together today. I heard them talking."

"What were they saying?" Maria asked quickly. Caroline thought that Maria had tensed up suddenly.

"Something about being glad that I hadn't found them out."

"Oh," Maria said, nearly smiling. She seemed to be digesting this for a minute, then she said in a kindly way, "You know, Cara, you've got this all wrong. There's nothing between Alex and Chrissy."

"Oh, sure," Caroline said. "I saw them, Maria."

"Just because you see two people together does not make them automatically engaged," Maria said.

"They were acting as if they were almost engaged," Caroline said. "How can they do this, Maria? My cousin and my boyfriend!"

"You're wrong, Cara. I know you're under a lot of pressure right now. When people are under too much pressure, they start imagining things that don't exist."

"Are you saying that I've finally flipped?" Caroline managed a weak smile.

Maria smiled back. "Of course not. I'm saying that you're worrying for nothing, just because you overheard a conversation. Did you actually hear your name being mentioned?"

"Well, no," Caroline admitted.

"So they could have been talking about anybody or anything, right?"

"I guess so."

"You see, you jumped to conclusions because you saw them talking together. They might have been having a good laugh about a teacher at school."

"Maybe," Caroline said. She took a deep breath and turned to Maria. "Look, Maria. You're my oldest friend. You'd tell me if you knew something was going on behind my back, wouldn't you?"

Maria looked at her steadily. "I'd tell you the minute you had something to worry about," she said. "And you don't. I'm around them all the time, Cara. I'd have noticed if any funny business was going on."

She put her hand on Caroline's shoulder. "Think of Alex, Caroline. He's one of the nicest guys I know. Do you think he'd two-time you? If he found somebody he liked better, he'd come right out and tell you about it and break up gently. He's the world's biggest Boy Scout! You know that."

"I guess you're right," Caroline admitted. "Alex isn't the sort of person I'd expect to cheat. He doesn't like hurting people."

"So stop worrying," Maria said. "Just forget about this whole thing until your performance is over. Then you'll realize that you were worrying over nothing."

At that moment the bell rang. Caroline and Maria

had to go in separate directions. Caroline walked to class in total confusion, her mind jumping back and forth between what she had seen and what Maria had said to her. All afternoon she thought of what she had seen, looking for clues that she was right or wrong. It had seemed so obvious, but neither Alex nor Chrissy had said anything definite.

Alex wouldn't two-time me. Maria is right, she tried telling herself. *If he wanted to break up, he'd come right out and say we should break up. But Maria didn't see what I saw.*

"Are you with us, Caroline Kirby?" her chemistry teacher asked sixth period, making Caroline jump from her seat. She wasn't usually the student who got picked on for daydreaming. She blushed scarlet and tried to concentrate, but her mind would not stop playing scenes of Chrissy and Alex. She pictured them together when they were arm-wrestling—the first time she had really suspected that they might be falling for each other. She saw Alex frantically chasing the bulldozer, she saw them sitting together on the front porch, Chrissy in her tiny bikini and Alex close beside her on the blanket.

Then she began to think of all the other suspicious occasions that she had been too naïve to notice. There had been a phone call a few evenings earlier:

"Was that the phone?" she had asked Chrissy, drying her hair as she came out of the bathroom. "Anyone for me?"

Chrissy had put down the receiver hastily. "Er, no, it wasn't for you at all," she had said. "It was for me.

Just the guys wanting to see if I was coming to the movie tonight."

"Another movie?" Caroline had asked. "All you guys seem to do these days is go to movies."

"Well, there are so many great ones playing right now, I don't want to miss any."

"So what masterpiece is playing this time?" Caroline had asked.

"It's . . . er . . . *The Return of the Spiderwoman*," Chrissy had mumbled.

Caroline had made some wisecrack then about American culture at its best and how much she was going to miss watching people having their blood sucked out. Then she had asked, "Is Alex going to the movie with you tonight?" and Chrissy had rushed away, mumbling about being late.

I bet they weren't going to a movie at all. I bet they were going out alone together. I never heard of The Return of the Spiderwoman.

Caroline realized she had not heard a word of what the chemistry teacher was saying. She glanced over to see what kind of notes the boy next to her was taking, but he was reading the newspaper, hiding it behind his textbook on the lab table. And there on the page was a huge ad for *The Return of the Spiderwoman. Maybe Maria is right,* she told herself. *Am I really cracking under pressure and reading things into innocent conversations?*

Caroline knew there was only one way to put all her worries to rest. She would have to confront Chrissy and Alex. The thought made her sick and scared. What if they told her she was right and they had fallen in love with each other? *How would I handle that?* Caroline wondered. *Living in an apartment with a girl who is dating my ex-boyfriend, having to watch him pick her up and drop her off, maybe walking to the front door just as he's kissing her good night. Wouldn't that be even worse than what I'm going through now?*

Her hand trembled as she tried to pour liquid into a test tube. *I don't want to lose Alex,* she thought. *At least if I don't know exactly what's going on, I can still hope. Maybe I can find a way to get him back again.*

The test tube slipped through Caroline's fingers, bounced off the edge of the table, fell to the floor, and shattered. Caroline jumped up guiltily. "I'm so sorry, Mrs. Hodges," she mumbled.

The teacher shook her head and smiled. "It's just not your day, is it, Caroline? That's okay. We all have bad days, and you're usually a hard worker. Go get this mess swept up and you can watch Danny's experiment. I don't think we can risk any more broken test tubes. Our budget is small enough as it is!"

Crimson with embarrassment, Caroline bent to sweep up the pieces of glass. *She's right about one thing,* she thought grimly. *It definitely is not my day! In fact today is so bad that I'd officially declare it tomorrow if tomorrow weren't the dance performance. I wish I could wake up and find it was next week, or next year, or even next life.*

Seventeen

Caroline lay awake in her darkened room, staring at the ceiling she could hardly see, every muscle of her body tense enough to snap. By the end of school, she had decided that Maria was right, that she was mistaken about Chrissy and Alex; the pressure of her ballet performance the next day was causing her to see everything at its worst. She had resolved to follow Maria's advice and forget everything else until her performance was finished.

Then she had met Justine in the parking lot after school.

"Are you waiting for Chrissy?" Justine had asked. "She asked me to tell you she's not walking home today. She has an errand to run, and she'll see you later."

Chrissy had not shown up at home by the time Caroline had left for dress rehearsal, and she was still not home when Caroline returned several hours later.

"She called to say something about going out with the gang to a movie," her mother said innocently. "Don't worry about her. I expect Alex will drive her home."

So Caroline had dragged herself to bed. Now she lay wide awake, waiting for Chrissy. One minute she told herself that she was being childish and unfair—Chrissy was indeed at a movie with the gang. The next minute her imagination flashed scenes of Alex and Chrissy together across her bedroom ceiling.

How could she? Caroline thought angrily. *To flaunt it like this the night before my big performance.*

Then the horrible thought occurred to her that perhaps something awful had happened to Chrissy, and she was flooded with guilt.

It was around twelve thirty when Caroline finally heard the sound of a car drawing up outside the house. Her heart beat furiously as she recognized the unmistakable pop-popping noise of Alex's Bug. The engine stopped. Caroline held her breath. After an eternity, a car door slammed and Chrissy's light steps padded toward the front door.

Chrissy turned the doorknob slowly and quietly and let herself into the bedroom. She tiptoed across the floor and put down her shoes on the throw rug by her bed.

"Is that you, Chrissy?" Caroline asked as Chrissy leaned toward the floor.

Chrissy jumped. "Sorry, Cara, did I wake you? I was trying to be quiet."

"I bet you were," Caroline said. "But it so happens that I wasn't asleep. I was too wound up after the dress rehearsal. I lay here going through all the mistakes I made in my mind. And when I'd finished going through my mistakes, I started wondering where my cousin could have gone and who she had gone with. . . ."

"Oh, that's easy," Chrissy said with a light little laugh. "A group of us just went out for ice cream after the movie and we started talking. You know how it is. . . ."

"I know that Mama's closes at ten-thirty," Caroline said dryly. "And I also happen to recognize the sound of my boyfriend's car when I hear it."

"So Alex gave me a ride home," Chrissy said. "What's wrong with that?"

"And he parked outside for quite a while before I heard your feet come up the steps."

"So, we were finishing a discussion," Chrissy said. "Why don't you go to sleep? We're both tired, I guess."

"I'm not stupid, Chrissy," Caroline said, propping herself up on her elbow and staring hard at her cousin in the dim light coming through the window. "I'm also not blind. You have been obviously flirting with Alex since you got here, and I guess it finally worked."

"Me, flirting with Alex? What are you talking about?"

"Oh, come on, Chrissy. I should have known what you were up to that first day I came home and watched you wiggling close to him in your itsy-bitsy bikini. And there have been lots of times since then when I have wondered what there was between you two. Now I guess I don't have to wonder anymore. I guess I just have to face the fact that my boyfriend has been two-timing me with a little farm girl from Iowa. How I'm going to live that down at school I don't know. I'll be a total laughingstock!"

"Caroline, you've got it all wrong!"

"Oh, I've got it all wrong," Caroline said in a polite, strained voice. "In that case, exactly where were you with my boyfriend until midnight? What exactly were you doing—and please don't lie about any crummy movie?"

"We just went out for a drive, Cara. And the car broke down on the way home."

"How convenient of it. Where did it break down, Chrissy?"

"In Golden Gate Park," Chrissy said with a gulp.

"So his car broke down," Caroline said. "And where were you heading to or heading from at this point?"

"It was just a drive, Caroline," Chrissy said wearily. "Nowhere special. I needed to talk to someone."

"So you chose Alex to talk to. Exactly what did you need to talk about?"

"Nothing special. I was feeling down, and Alex is a good listener, that's all."

"Sure he is," Caroline said bitterly. "I can see you right now, fluttering your eyelashes and lisping: 'Oh, Alex, poor little me all alone with no one to look after me here. Gee, you're so big and strong and wonderful.' I've seen you at school, Chrissy. You are the world's biggest flirt!"

"Me? A flirt? Are you crazy? I never flirt! I can't stand flirts."

"Then it must have been your double who was teasing strange boys in the halls."

"That's not flirting! I only answer people when they speak to me. We trade insults. It's totally harmless."

"Not when you don't know the boy. Nobody around here calls out after strange boys. That is totally uncivilized."

"So you think I'm uncivilized?"

"Well, let me put it to you this way. It might be okay in Iowa to steal another girl's boy, but it's not okay in California."

"You've got it wrong, Caroline," Chrissy said in a small voice. "I haven't been trying to steal your boyfriend. I'm sorry if you can't believe that, but it's the truth."

"Oh, sure," Caroline said, sitting up in bed and hugging her knees to her. "I can think of a million and one innocent things that you could have been doing together at midnight! It's just not fair, Chrissy. I'm under all this pressure to perform in a ballet I'm not really ready for, and you're going behind my back the night before my performance.

"I'm not, Cara!" Chrissy pleaded.

"You've been doing it ever since you got here," Caroline went on, ignoring Chrissy's plea. "First it was playing up to my parents until they thought you were wonderful and I was lazy and useless. Then you started on my friends! I introduced you to people so that you wouldn't be lonely all year. But you couldn't stand for them to be my friends, too, so you've tried to take my place!"

"Cara, how could you say that?" Chrissy asked, her voice trembling. "That's just not true."

"Oh, no? Then what about all the secret little phone calls to Justine and Tracy. You're always hanging up the phone just as I come into the room, and going off to movies when you *know* I have rehearsals. You may fool other people, but you don't fool me. I think you're a creep, Chrissy. I wish you'd never come here. I'm going to sleep now. I've got a performance tomorrow, and I don't want to make a fool of myself, screwing up in front of all those people, so I'm going to *try* to get some rest."

Caroline lay down in bed and turned her back on Chrissy without another word. Chrissy walked slowly to her side of the room. "Good night, Caroline," she said. She undressed in silence and climbed into bed. It was a long time before Caroline finally fell asleep.

In the morning, Caroline got up without even looking in Chrissy's direction. She showered and ate breakfast like a zombie and was about to leave the house for her final rehearsal when she caught sight of a half-written letter lying on Chrissy's bed. She could hear the water going for Chrissy's shower.

The first lines of the letter leaped up at her in Chrissy's big, childish handwriting:

Dear Ben,

I'm so homesick I don't know what to do. I'll never fit in here if I stay for a million years. I've messed things up with Caroline, and she hates me now. . .

Caroline turned away angrily and ran out of the house. Had that girl no shame at all? How could she spend the evening with Alex and then write to her boyfriend as if nothing were going on? A guilty thought crossed her mind that maybe Chrissy was telling the truth about the evening with Alex, but she tossed it aside angrily. *She's playing up to Ben now, for his sympathy, just the way she played up to my parents and my friends and then Alex. She's just a great big phony who acts helpless to get what she wants!*

Caroline ran all the way to dance practice as if she wanted to put as much distance between her and Chrissy as possible. All through warm-up exercises, her legs felt heavy as lead and her arms stiff and jerky as if she hadn't used any of her limbs in a long while.

"Relax, Caroline," her ballet teacher commanded. "I can see the tension. Let it flow. You'll do beautifully tonight—there is no need for nerves."

"Oh, sure," Caroline muttered to herself. "No need for nerves. It seems like I've already lost everything else I care about. This performance is the only thing I have left. If I wreck this, I might as well give up."

After rehearsal, Caroline walked the long way home. It was a windy day, with a hint of fall in the air. Clouds were scudding across the Marin hills and the bay was full of white caps. A few yachts brave enough to risk the weather were flying across the water, at impossible angles.

Guilt began to nag at Caroline. She had been tired and tense the night before. She had said a lot of terrible things to Chrissy. Maybe she had blown things out of proportion. But Chrissy hadn't even defended herself. She hadn't lost her own temper and argued with Caroline. She had just crept into bed. *That must prove her guilt,* Caroline decided. *If anyone accused me of something totally false, I'd get really upset. But she didn't. She stayed calm and just turned away.*

Caroline closed her eyes to try to shut out the image of Chrissy and Alex together. Of course he'd be attracted to Chrissy. Who wouldn't have been? She was pretty and bright and she refused to take life too seriously. Not like Caroline, who shut herself away like a clam and worried all the time about living up to everyone else's expectations. Perhaps Caroline needed to be more like Chrissy sometimes. What was the point of trying to please everyone else all of the time if someone else who never stopped to worry about whom she pleased ran ahead of you, grabbing everything you wanted?

The wind along the marina was so strong it took Caroline's breath away and stung her cheeks. She turned and walked toward home again. It wouldn't help matters any to catch pneumonia and miss her recital. Besides, now that she had sorted out the situation mentally, it would be easier to face Chrissy. But Chrissy wasn't even home when Caroline got there.

"She left about a half hour ago with Alex," her father said, not thinking anything was wrong with that statement. "She didn't say where they were going!"

So I wasn't wrong, Caroline thought bleakly. *Even though she knows I've got an important performance today, even though she knows how much it means to me, and how nervous about it I've been, she still goes off with my boyfriend. I bet they don't even bother to show up tonight. Well, that's okay, I don't think I want those two to be there when I dance!*

Eighteen

It was ten minutes before curtain time, and the small dressing room was buzzing like a beehive with excited whispers. Most of the girls crowded around the big mirror, elbowing their way to a little patch of glass. Caroline stood alone in a corner, trying to pin her head-dress in place without the help of her reflection. The smell of greasepaint and the rustle of the tutus reminded her of her first ballet recitals, when the dressing room was always crowded with proud mothers, all putting the finishing touches to their daughters. Now the dancers were in a real performing company. No one would have allowed her mother beyond the dressing room door. This wasn't just a little show for parents and friends, but a real performance for the public, in a big, formal theater. She stuck another pin through her crown of flowers and wished for a moment that her mother *were* there to dress her and to fix her makeup with that last soft, warm pat of the powder puff, the way she always had done before.

"Do you need a hand with that, Caroline?" Darcy, a petite redhead, asked behind her. "I'm all done with mine, and I'm so nervous I just can't bear to stand around doing nothing."

"Thanks," Caroline said. "I can't seem to stop it from sticking up at the back."

"I know. Mine took a whole box of bobby pins. I'll probably scatter them all over the stage every time I leap. It'll sound like machine-gun fire!"

Caroline grinned. "As long as the headdress doesn't fall off. That would be the most embarrassing thing, wouldn't it?"

"No," Darcy said. "The most embarrassing thing would be for the tutu to fall off!" They both giggled, and Caroline felt the warmth of shared worry. It was comforting to have someone beside her who understood why she was so nervous.

"You're so lucky," Darcy went on. "You never seem to get scared or upset like I do. You're always so calm about things. Even when Madame yells. My legs are trembling so much I can hardly stand up some nights, but you just keep right on dancing."

"Me?" Caroline asked in surprise. "But I thought I was the only one who was terrified. Everyone else seems so cool."

"You always look like you're cool," Darcy admitted. "I always look like I'm about to cry. I can feel these pink spots growing on my cheeks. But I think we all learned how to handle Madame pretty well, don't you?

From now on, we just smash her banana—we show her we'll take no nonsense from her!"

Darcy broke off as Madame's voice boomed through the dressing room. "Let me take a look at you, girls! Turn around . . . there. You look beautiful, all of you. I know you will dance divinely tonight. You will float as lightly as butterflies and make me proud of you!" She turned to go. "On stage in five minutes. And remember, you are now dancers. No talking backstage. You behave like professionals." Then she swept out.

"What were you saying about Madame?" Caroline whispered with a grin to Darcy.

Darcy grinned back. "I take it all back," she whispered. "She still terrifies me. Let's go onstage and peek through to see if our folks are here yet."

"I don't think we're supposed to do that," Caroline said hesitantly. "Madame would think that was unprofessional."

"Madame won't see," Darcy said. "I'm dying to see if my boyfriend's sitting near the front. If I can see him when I dance, I know I'll mess up. I told him to sit way at the back." She dragged Caroline down the cold hallway and out onto the stage. It looked immense with only two people on it. The murmured conversations of the audience drifted through the curtain. Darcy found the center and peeked through.

"I see him," she whispered. "He's near the back, thank heavens. Now I won't have to worry about seeing his face when the lights go out. There's my mom. And she brought Derrick, her latest boyfriend. I don't know what he wants to see ballet for. His culture usually doesn't stretch past Monday Night Football. I bet Mom made him come!" She giggled and turned back to Caroline. "You want to look now?"

Caroline felt her heart flutter. She had no idea what she would find beyond the curtain.

"I don't think so," she said, glancing around nervously. More girls were starting to drift onstage. But she couldn't resist. How wonderful it would be to look out and find Alex's face shining up at her. "Okay, just one quick peek then." She peered out through the tiny slit. The hall was gigantic—and filled with row after row of faces. She knew more or less where the seats were that she had reserved for her parents and friends and counted back toward them. Yes, there was her father. She could see his glasses reflecting the ceiling lights. And her mother was right beside him. But to her right stood a whole empty row of chairs. No Tracy, no Justine, no Alex or Chrissy or anybody.

Great, she thought. *They couldn't even make it to my first performance on time. Maybe they're not even coming at all. Maybe they have another movie to go to. Some friends they turned out to be.*

She turned away from the curtains, sorry she had bothered to look. "My parents are here," she said. "We'd better get in our places."

She took up her position, kneeling on one knee while Tanya leaned on her shoulder in an arabesque. The taped music began to play—orchestras cost too much for a small local company, but at least tonight the sound came through the theater's PA system. Caroline could feel Tanya's hand trembling on her shoulder.

I don't care if nobody's here, she decided. *I'm going*

to dance as I've never danced before, even if nobody watches me.

The curtains opened, and there was a large burst of applause as the audience admired the tableau of lilac tutus and flowered headdresses. Caroline rose, extended her arms and moved into her place in the line. She could feel the electricity flowing through them all. The music built toward its climax, and she began to dance. No longer was she conscious of right feet and wrong feet, of her position in the line, of the way she held her arms. She was not Caroline, carrying out a ballet exercise for her teacher. She was a dancer, moving to music that filled her soul. She was as light as a feather, as graceful as a doe, as beautiful and delicate as a butterfly.

This is what it was all about, she thought. *This moment makes it all worth it. I'm a real dancer in a real ballet!*

Amazingly quickly it was over. The dance seemed only to have lasted moments; yet, as they posed in their final tableau and then walked forward to curtsy, Caroline noticed the sweat trickling down her face and arms. The applause went on. They curtsyed a second time, then the curtain fell. Madame was everywhere at once, rushing to congratulate first one student then the next.

Caroline wandered back to the dressing room in a daze. All around her the other girls were rapidly chatting, commenting in horror about the number of times they did something wrong or missed a cue or got out of line and whether Madame had noticed. Caroline realized then with an overwhelming sense of relief that she hadn't made a single awful mistake. She had kept her position in line, she had managed all those difficult turns without colliding with anyone, and her ankle had not even wobbled on the arabesque. It was all over, and she had done it. Then, mingled with her relief came the disappointment that none of her friends—none of the people she thought were her friends—had come to share her success.

Family and friends were bursting in through the dressing room door now, hugging their stars and presenting flowers. Caroline took off her makeup quietly in the farthest corner, and slowly untied her ballet shoes. She was too modest to want to take off her tutu in front of so many strangers, so she wrapped her robe around her, gathered her clothes, and headed for the bathrooms to change. She pushed past the crowd at the door—and there was Alex, standing alone in the hallway, half-hidden behind a huge bouquet of long-stemmed red roses. Caroline stopped short when she saw him.

"Oh, Alex," she said. Her voice would not behave normally.

A big grin spread across Alex's face. "Oh, there you are, Cara," he said. "Boy, am I glad you came out. I was going to try and come in, but there are all sorts of undressed women in there, and you know what a sheltered life I've led!" He stepped forward awkwardly. "Here, these are for you."

Caroline took the bouquet with an embarrassed smile. "From you? All these flowers?" she stammered.

"Not just from me. From all your friends. We thought you were great, Cara."

"Oh, jeepers," Caroline said, realizing as she said it that she sounded just like Chrissy.

"I think I'll wait outside, if you don't mind," Alex said, as one half-clad girl ran past him down the hall. "Hurry up and get changed, and I'll drive you home."

"My parents are waiting out front," Caroline said uncertainly. This was not at all how she imagined she'd be spending the evening, and a thousand unasked questions were colliding in her brain. "I expect they'll want to drive me home."

"I told them I'd drive you," Alex said. "They already went. I wanted a few minutes with you to myself."

"You did?" Caroline asked hesitantly. "What about Chrissy?"

"Chrissy?" Alex asked. "Chrissy already got a ride home with your folks. It's just the two of us."

"And is that what you really want?" Caroline asked.

Alex looked at her steadily. "I want to be alone with my girlfriend for a while," he said. "Is that okay with you?"

"If you're sure that's what you want," Caroline said.

"Look, Cara," Alex said gently. "We haven't had too much time for each other recently, and I haven't had a chance to tell you how proud I am of you and how all your hard work paid off." He reached across and touched her arm. "You were great, Cara. I couldn't believe it was you up there on the stage. You really are a ballerina. . . ." He stopped and laughed awkwardly. "But then I guess you already knew that, didn't you?"

"No," Caroline said, her eyes shining. "I didn't know it until tonight. Thank you, Alex."

Alex looked around him. "Come on, let's get out of here," he said.

"What's the big hurry?"

"Everybody's hugging everybody."

"What's wrong with that?"

"I don't want to be hugged by some strange girl," he said. "Maybe later, when we're alone, we can get in a little hugging."

"I guess we should go straight home," Caroline said wistfully. "My parents will be waiting."

"Fine with me," Alex said. "We'll go straight home. Now hurry up and get dressed!"

Fifteen minutes later they climbed the stairs to Caroline's apartment.

"My legs are so tired I can hardly make it," Caroline complained.

"In which case," Alex said casually, "maybe you'd like a little help." Without waiting for her answer, he swept her up into his arms and carried her up the rest of the stairs.

"Here we are, star ballerina and escort!" he yelled, kicking the door open before them. He lowered Caroline gently to the ground, watching in delight as disbelief spread over her face. Streamers were festooned across the walls and ceiling. Bunches of pink-and-white balloons were clustered in the corners. A long banner across the fireplace proclaimed in gold letters, "Congratulations, Caroline!" The dining room table and its pink-and-white tablecloth were almost hidden beneath piles of chips, dips, veggies, and cold cuts. In the middle, a huge punch bowl steamed mysteriously like a witch's brew, and on a cut-glass stand next to it stood a perfect ballet slipper of pink frosting.

Caroline stood still, her mouth open, looking first at the room, then at Alex.

"Did you do all this?" she asked finally.

Alex smiled. "I had a little help," he said. "You can come out now, guys."

"Surprise!" came a great roar of voices as Caroline's friends burst out of the kitchen and living room where they had been hiding.

"Congratulations, Cara," Tracy yelled, hugging Caroline.

"Your dancing was wonderful," Justine added. Her best friends clustered around her, hugging her and laughing and crying. From their midst Caroline looked up and saw Chrissy standing apart from the crowd. She broke away from the group and walked over to her.

"Congratulations, Cara," Chrissy said hesitantly.

"Were you part of all this?" Caroline asked. Chrissy nodded.

"Part of it?" Alex added. "She thought of it. It was her idea, because she wanted to cheer you up and she wanted you to know how proud we all were of you."

Caroline went on looking at Chrissy. "And all those evenings you kept going out and all those times you hung up the phone when I came into the room, you were arranging this, right?"

"Right," Chrissy said.

"I feel like a fool, Chrissy," Caroline said. "I said some horrible things to you. No wonder you didn't defend yourself. You couldn't, without giving the whole secret away. Will you ever forgive me?"

"Of course, I'll forgive you," Chrissy said. "I would have probably jumped to the same conclusion twice as fast if it had been me."

"No, you wouldn't," Caroline said. "You're much too nice."

"Are you joking?" Chrissy asked. "My dad says I have the world's worst temper, and heaven help any girl I find fooling around with Ben."

She slipped her arm through Caroline's. "Come on, I bet you're dying of thirst. Try Maria's magic punch."

Caroline allowed herself to be led toward the food table. "It's all so beautiful," she commented. "Especially that cake shaped like a ballet slipper! I can't get over it."

"That was the item that caused all the trouble," Chrissy said with a grin. "We had ordered it from a special bakery, and we had to pick it up last night out on the Avenues. It was on the way back from there that the car broke down in Golden Gate Park. I figured you'd be asleep, and I didn't think of a good excuse to tell you about where we'd been."

"I've been a suspicious old grouch," Caroline admitted, taking a long drink of punch.

"You never should have suspected Alex," Chrissy said. "He's crazy about you! You should have known that he'd never go behind your back."

"I've always felt so insecure," Caroline said, playing with her napkin, unable to meet Chrissy's look. "I've spent half my life trying to be what people want me to be and the other half worrying that they won't like me if

I fail. I really envy you, Chrissy. You're happy just to be yourself. You say what you really feel, and you don't act phony, and you laugh at yourself if you make a mistake. And everybody loves you for it."

"That doesn't mean I feel any more at ease with people than you do," Chrissy said. "I'm still scared about fitting in with new people, and I'm still embarrassed when I do something dumb, believe it or not. It's because of my pride that I'd rather be the one to start the laughter. I can't stand the thought of being laughed at behind my back."

Caroline nodded as if she understood, but she couldn't imagine acting so bravely. "You're a very strong person," she said.

"Who, me?" Chrissy laughed, shaking her head in disbelief. "You're the strong person. You push yourself hard to succeed. You go to all these dance practices, and then you sit for hours at your desk doing homework. Me, I'm a flake. If the homework looks too hard, I get someone to help me, or I go out to the movies and pretend it will go away."

The girls walked together across the room.

"I've got to do some serious thinking," Caroline said. "I put too much pressure on myself, I know that. One day I'll snap."

Chrissy nodded wisely. "Maybe you'll have to convince yourself that it's okay not to please everybody all the time. It's not failing, it's impossible. Everybody will still like you. The world won't fall to pieces."

Caroline looked at Chrissy with understanding. "You're right," she said. "I like being best at what I do—tonight I felt like I could touch the moon. But the world wouldn't fall to pieces if I messed up in my next ballet, or I got a B on a test. And I think I learned tonight that the only person I really have to please is me: If I feel good about myself, then that's all that matters, isn't it?"

Chrissy looked at her seriously. "Well —you could think about pleasing your cousin, too, by tasting that dip it took me hours to make," she said.

Caroline laughed and dipped in a cauliflower floweret. "Mmm," she said in appreciation. "Old Iowa recipe?"

"Oh, yeah. Back of a soup box!" Chrissy confessed. The girls laughed together. Caroline took a plate and began piling it with food.

"From now on I'm going to try to stop worrying and enjoy life more, just like you," she said, "starting right now. I'm going to fill myself a plate of all that delicious food, and then I'm going to put on loud music and find Alex and dance all night!"

Nineteen

Early Sunday morning Chrissy and Caroline finally said good-bye to the last guests and crawled into their beds. Strangely enough, Caroline didn't feel at all tired anymore. She lay on top of her covers, too pleased and excited to get undressed and climb into bed. She stared at the ceiling, picturing every detail of the evening again: Alex waiting with the huge bouquet, the decorated room, the guests bursting out from all sides, Chrissy hanging back shyly—and finally, wandering alone with Alex down to the porch.

"So now that you're a full-fledged ballerina, does that mean I'm going to see even less of you?" he had asked, with a smile on his face but in a very solemn voice.

"I'm going to try really hard, Alex," Caroline said. "To get my life in order, I mean. I'm going to try and make more time to have fun with my friends and especially to be with you. We don't have another performance until spring, so I won't have all those horrible extra rehearsals for a while."

"But what if the New York City Ballet saw you tonight and decides to draft you?" Alex asked.

Caroline laughed. "You don't draft ballet dancers—that's football players," she said. "Besides, I know I'm not good enough to be recruited by a big ballet company. I'm the same as everyone else, if I practice really hard. I'm not outstanding."

"To me you are," Alex said. "You looked incredible to me."

"You're prejudiced," Caroline said, smiling at him tenderly. "And anyway, even if the New York City Ballet did want me, I wouldn't go. I'm not ready to go anywhere yet. I have too many things I don't want to leave behind." She reached out and stroked his cheek.

"Things?" Alex teased. "You think of me as a thing?"

"People, too," Caroline corrected. "I have too many people I would miss very badly. Too many people I can't do without."

Alex slid his arms around her waist. "I'm glad you can't do without me," he whispered. "Because I hate it when you're not around. Nothing's the same when you're not there, Cara. I like all of our friends a lot, but we need time to ourselves if our relationship is going to grow."

Caroline wrapped her arms around his neck. "We'll make time, Alex," she said. "We'll make a firm date, every week, to spend one evening on our own, just the two of us."

"That's great, Cara," Alex said. "I was beginning to think I'd have to join the ballet company to be able to talk to you, and I'd look terrible in pink tights!"

Caroline giggled. "I don't know," she said, "you look cute on the soccer field in those little shorts. I bet you'd look great in tights."

Alex's grip tightened around her. "Oh, Cara," he said. "I've missed you so much lately. We haven't had time to talk and laugh together for so long. I felt rotten after our fight. I was wrong to come down so hard on you. I should have realized how much pressure you were under."

"I *did* overreact," Caroline said, gazing at him steadily. "It's just that life has been so serious lately, so full of expectations and demands. It never occurred to me that you might be doing something nice for me." Caroline sighed. "Chrissy has the right idea about things. She doesn't take anything too seriously. She doesn't seem to worry at all—"

"Maybe she's just found the right way to deal with her problems," Alex suggested. "Everything hasn't been so great for her here."

"Chrissy?" Caroline asked, surprised. "What problems could she have had? She's never mentioned anything to me."

"Maybe it's not so easy for her to talk to you. Sharing a room with somebody or being her cousin doesn't automatically make you best friends," Alex said. "You two need to get to know each other better. Of course, I don't want you and Chrissy to be such good friends that you forget about me. I'm always there when you need me, Cara. All you have to do is call."

"You're sweet, Alex," Caroline said. "I'm really glad you're here."

"Me, too," Alex said as he bent to kiss her.

Caroline smiled to herself as she lay on her bed remembering the warmth of that kiss. "Chrissy?" she asked. "Are you still awake?"

"I don't think I'll be able to sleep tonight," Chrissy said. "I'm too wound up."

"Me, too," Caroline said. "It was a wonderful party, Chrissy. I'm so glad you had the idea. Everything was just perfect."

"I'm glad you liked it, Cara," Chrissy said. "It was the biggest party I was ever in charge of. It's nice to know that the organizational skills I learned helping out at Iowa church socials can pay off in sophisticated San Francisco."

Caroline sat up. "You want to go and make some hot chocolate?" she asked. "That might help us get to sleep."

"I'm not sure if I could cram another thing into my stomach, but I'm willing to try," Chrissy said. Together they crept to the kitchen.

"It's kind of nice to have someone to share a hot chocolate with in the middle of the night," Caroline said as she handed Chrissy a cup of the steaming liquid. "When you're used to a big family, I expect you take things like that for granted."

"Are you joking?" Chrissy asked. "My brothers would kill me if I tried to wake them up in the middle of the night! It's bad enough trying to get them out of bed in the mornings for school. You have to grab Tom by the feet and drag him out from under the covers." She smiled wistfully.

"You really miss them, don't you?" Caroline asked.

Chrissy nodded. "Sometimes I miss them so much it really hurts. I have to hold myself back from rushing to the phone and calling them."

"Why don't you?"

"Because I know it would be worse once I put the phone down and realized that they were so far away and out of reach."

"I had no idea," Caroline said thoughtfully. "It never occurred to me that it would be so hard for you. I thought it would be such fun for you to be in a city like San Francisco, and you seemed to adjust so well. You make friends so easily; you're always going places and doing things. I really envied the way you could fit in with no problems."

Chrissy laughed. "If you only knew what was going through my head," she said. "I've been feeling so homesick that the only way I could shut it out was by keeping myself busy. I've been trying to fill every minute with something to do just to avoid thinking about home. That's how Alex and I came up with the idea for the party for you. When he found me crying one night, I told him how homesick I was. He suggested I do something really useful and important to me instead of just going from one bad movie to the next."

"And I never realized," Caroline said. "I sat home full of envy because you were out having a good time while I was stuck at home working. You really covered up your homesickness well. Why didn't you tell me?"

Chrissy looked embarrassed. "Because I didn't think you'd understand," she said. "You always seemed so cool—so in charge of your emotions. I thought someone who was bored with Europe would think I was stupid to be homesick for Iowa. I thought you'd just look down on me even more."

"Oh, Chrissy," Caroline said. "If you only knew . . . there are so many things I'm good at hiding, including the way I feel most of the time. I only said I was bored with Europe because my parents couldn't afford to send me with the others this year, and it hurt to watch them all going without me. If I acted like I looked down on you, maybe it was because I felt threatened by you—I envied you because you never seem to worry about the things that bothered me."

Chrissy smiled. "We lived in the same house for more than a month, and we didn't know anything about each other, really. We both thought the other one had it so easy. I was scared to talk to you because I thought you wouldn't care about such boring problems".

"And I was scared because I wasn't used to telling other people how I felt," Caroline said. "When you've been an only child all your life, you grow up to be a very private person, I guess." She got up and walked across the kitchen, holding the warm mug cupped in her hands. "I'm sorry if I treated you badly, Chrissy. The truth is, the idea of your coming to live here wasn't easy for me either. I know you've had to go through homesickness and starting off in a new school, and those things are hard, but sharing my room and my parents has been hard for me—and sharing my friends, too, I guess. I'm used to having a lot of privacy and time for myself."

"I understand," Chrissy said. "I felt the same way, I guess, as if I never had a place to go and be alone and catch up on my own thoughts. I do have a big family, but since I'm the only girl, I always had my own room and plenty of space."

"You, too?" Caroline asked. Then she burst out laughing. "It's amazing. We were both going through the same things, and we never knew. We could have made it so much easier for ourselves if we'd just come right out and talked about what was bugging us." Caroline hesitated. "Like the way you leave your clothes all over everything."

Chrissy made a face. "I know. I'm a terrible slob," she said. "My mom's always yelling at me at home about it. I'll try harder if you try not to spend so long in the bathroom."

Caroline was horrified. "Me? I spend too long in the bathroom? I do not!"

"You try being the second person who also has to get ready for school," Chrissy suggested. "By the time I get in there, there's just enough hot water left for a three-minute shower, which is all the time I've got then, anyway!"

"Well, at least I don't leave my wet towel on the bedroom floor for other people to pick up!" Caroline protested.

"No, but you take up the whole shelf with your makeup!"

"I do not."

"Do, too!"

"Hey, what's going on in here?" Caroline's father asked, poking his head around the door. "Are you guys fighting or partying?"

"Neither," Caroline said. "We're just being two siblings, acting the way siblings always act. You've gotten off easy as a parent so far because there's just been me, but now you're going to find out what it's like in real families where the people act like normal kids!"

"Heaven spare us," Mr. Kirby said, rolling his eyes upward, but smiling at the same time. "In that case, could you please put off the sibling rivalry until morning? Your mother and I have to get some sleep to be prepared for what's coming."

He turned and walked out of the kitchen. Caroline looked at Chrissy and began to laugh. Then Chrissy burst out laughing, too. They gave each other a giant hug and stood laughing and crying together in the kitchen.

"Cara, I'm really glad I'm here," Chrissy said at last. "All my life I've wanted a sister. Now, at least, I've got one."

"I'm glad you're here, too," Caroline said. "We're going to have such a great year together—so much fun. We'll go to the Halloween parties in the city and skiing in the mountains and down to Hollywood—"

"*Mon Dieu*, I can hardly wait," Chrissy interrupted.

Caroline faked a look of shock. Then a broad grin crept across her face.

"Holy mazoley, neither can I," she said.

Here's a sneak preview from *Trading Places*, book number two of SUGAR & SPICE:

Chrissy reached for the finished pages of her letter as a gust swept in through the open window. But the wind lifted the pages off the ledge, and before she could catch them, they fluttered out into the darkness of the street below.

"Oh, jeepers!" Chrissy cried, leaping up and peering out. In the patches of light shining from the windows of the apartments below, she thought she spotted her letter partially hidden in a bush.

She hesitated for a moment, staring out at the deserted street. Then, after carefully making sure the door of the apartment was unlocked, Chrissy squinted down the two flights of stairs, past the front porch, and around to the side of the house, where she retrieved the two sheets of papers from the bush.

She was just returning to the porch when the wind whipped up again. Chrissy ran for the house, but she wasn't quick enough. The building's front door slammed shut in her face, leaving her shivering on the porch outside.

She tried the door, but it was firmly locked. "Holy mazoley," she sighed, bringing her hands up to her cheeks. Another gust of wind blew up from the wharf, and Chrissy felt her skin prickle with goose bumps. She was dressed only in her pink baby-doll pajamas, and nobody was home in the apartment to let her back in.

I could always sit on the porch until the others get home, she thought. *The concert will be over pretty soon*. Then she reconsidered. Sometimes Caroline's family went to a reception after the concert. *Do I wait around on the porch until after midnight?* she asked herself.

Then she noticed the bougainvillea. The huge vine climbed over one side of the porch and made its way up the side of the house.

Should I? Chrissy thought. She certainly didn't doubt her climbing ability. Her brother had once dared her to climb through her bedroom window back home at the farm by way of the big, old cottonwood tree. She'd had to walk along a limb of the trees then reach across to her window.

She glanced up and down the street. For once, there was nobody in sight on the sidewalk, and the cars sped past too quickly to see her. Chrissy swung herself onto the creeper and began to climb.

The trunk was huge and twisted into convenient footholds at the bottom. When Chrissy reached the top of the porch, she paused to catch her breath and look around. Above her she could see her own window, wide open and within easy reach. The only obstacle was the window on the floor below hers. It was open, and the light was on. Chrissy tried to remember who lived in the second-floor apartment, but she didn't think she'd ever met her downstairs neighbor.

"With any luck," she told herself as she inched upward again, "nobody will even notice that I'm—"

At that moment the piece of vine she was reaching for tore loose from the wall. Chrissy yelled as she swung away from the house. She put a hand out and grabbed a firmer branch. Her heart pounded so loudly she was sure that the sound echoed back from the house next door. Then she looked up. A face peered down from the second-floor window, only a few inches above her. Both she and the face screamed at the same time, then the window slammed shut and the face disappeared.

Chrissy clung to the vine. She considered lowering herself to the ground, but getting down didn't look so easy as getting up. She waited for the face to reappear in the window, so she could have a chance to explain—maybe the face would even invite her inside—but nothing moved behind the glass pane.

Then Chrissy heard a car screech to a stop in front

of the house. She turned to look, but she was blinded by a brilliant red light.

"Stay where you are!" a voice commanded. "If you don't move, nobody will get hurt."

"Oh, jeepers," Chrissy said out loud.

ABOUT THE AUTHOR

Janet Quin-Harkin is the author of more than thirty books for young adults, including the best-selling *Ten-Boy Summer* and *On Our Own*, its sequel series. Ms. Quin-Harkin lives just outside of San Francisco with her husband, three teenage daughters, and one son.

Janet
Quin-Harkin's
Sugar & Spice